Two Wrongs

Baron Alexander

Wilderwick Press

Forest Row, UK

Dedicated to Jack

CONTENTS

CHAPTER ONE

LAZARUS
United States
25 June 2025

Mark Burton stepped into the brilliant morning sunshine, squinting as he adjusted his eyes from the darker interior of his apartment building to the wide expanse of green, blue, and black before him. He noticed things like this now because he was glad to be alive. The last decade of his life was spent in a coma, where his muscles wasted and his body was monitored and kept alive despite the long odds against his recovery. *One hell of a diet regime*, he would tell people, but inwardly he wouldn't recommend it to anyone. He was weak, tired, and in need of rebuilding his muscles and his life.

He felt the compression of the soles of his shoes under his weight as he stepped off the curb onto the almost oily black tarmacadam road. He imagined a similar compression in his bones as he moved up and down, left and right, swaying naturally in a practiced lope called walking. He didn't have a swagger, but he was once athletic and intended to become so again. His body would just need to catch up.

"On your own today, Mark?" The building's porter was friendly with all of the residents. He held his take-away coffee and a brown bag containing his morning bran muffin from Joey's coffee shop around the corner.

"Yep. No more physio, but the docs say I need to stay active."

"Take it easy out there." The porter's words were genuine as he walked past Mark and up the manicured sidewalk into the front entrance of the complex. He disappeared inside and Mark returned to his task.

One foot in front of the other, he thought. As his foot touched the road, he felt a stab in his heart. It was the pain of loss remembered. Helen, his girlfriend at the time of his accident, had given up waiting for him to wake up after six months. She found someone from England and moved there. He heard she had a family now, two girls from her husband's previous marriage and one boy together with her new man. She contacted him shortly after he woke up. They talked, cried, and dealt with the guilt—hers, mainly. Mark reassured her he would have done the same, but he didn't believe it. He knew he needed to let her go and she needed to have reassurance that she was not a bad person. *Life sucks*, he thought as he refocussed on the present.

Mark's new Nike shoes seemed to grip exceptionally well. He felt the tension on his knees and joints when he turned his body. His feet didn't pivot. Unless he picked up and put down his foot in a new position, they were anchored to the newly laid road. He liked this sensation. It made him feel safe. He enjoyed the certainty of being planted to the earth. Every sensation was heightened, making him feel more alive now than at any point in his life.

He could just make out the smell of grilled food over the distinct aroma of freshly cut grass. A man was still cutting it not too far away. He looked for the tell-tale plume of smoke rising from a neighbour's BBQ but couldn't see anything. It made his mouth water and he carefully started walking in the direction of the local shops. There was a deli, Italian, with cheeses and olives and meats that made him hungry just thinking about it. He wanted a good pasta, full of cream and parmesan, to help build up his body. He needed to eat. He would start with some light cheese with tomatoes and olives and finish with some hard cheese and coffee. The pasta would be his main course and complete the meal. Or he might have the meatballs. Or the Parma ham. He never knew what he was going to eat until he actually ordered. He would hover in front of the curved glass, eyeing the food, pacing from end to end. Sometimes, he would see the person in front of him order something new and decide he wanted the same.

"Hi Mark, how're you doing today?" It was a girl of around thirty, in a bit of a hurry in the opposite direction. She slowed down when she neared.

"Hi Jenny," Mark said. "Doing okay. You?"

"Can't complain. Normal stuff. Good to see you out on your own." She cocked her head and smiled as if she was admiring a painting or watching a child swim for the first time. Mark couldn't tell if it was admiration or pity.

"Yeah, thanks. Good to be out. Just trying to exercise the old bones."

"Oh," she said, startled. "I forgot. I've got to go. By the way, did you hear the news?"

"No," Mark said. "Anything exciting?"

"Find a TV. It's on every station."

"What's up? Sounds ominous."

"Massive terrorist attack. Bastards. I'm just heading home to hug my kids and call my friends. You take care of yourself, Mark." She carried on down the street. He didn't have a chance to say anything further.

Bizarre, he thought. He was still a bit of a celebrity and people wondered at his miraculous waking, as they called it. He was a modern day Lazarus and when people saw him, they struck up a conversation. Today was no different.

"Did you see what those bastard rag heads did now? Someone should kill 'em all." A guy started talking to him without prompting. Mark didn't remember his name but recognised the face.

"What happened?"

"Those assholes blew up hundreds of planes all around the world. Just happened. Not sure about the details."

"Do we know who did it?" he asked.

"Not yet, but who else could it be?" said the man. "As the saying goes, not all Arabs are terrorists, but all terrorists are Arabs. My money's on the Ay-Rabs." He pronounced it like George Bush did after 9/11.

Mark shook his head. He remembered that day in September so long ago. The day that changed the course of US history and ideas of security around the world. Ordinary people were forced to endure extensive searches and invasions of their privacy. No phone call, email, or text was free from their listening ears and prying eyes. The governments tried to pretend as though everything was the same, but it wasn't. Then in 2017 or, more precisely, December 31, 2016, none of this mattered anymore for Mark. That was when he was crossing the road with then-girlfriend Helen on the way to their next party. She had dropped something from her purse and realised it when they reached the curb. Trying to be gallant, he leapt back into the road to retrieve the fallen treasure when he found himself face to face with the grill of a 1974 Mustang going flat out with no chance to stop or swerve. He spent the next decade in a coma. When he awoke, he was told the treasure he almost died for was a pack of gum.

Mark took the news of this most recent terrorist attack in stride. Most likely Jenny and this guy were over-reacting. Whatever the truth of the matter, his life wouldn't change. He was too old and beaten up for military service and too young to retire. He had a little money from the insurance policy but that just ensured a roof over his head and enough for three meals a day. He decided to continue to the deli. He was hungry and Luigi's had good food.

∞

"Hi Mark," said Luigi, smiling. "Nice to see you out and about. I guess you heard the news?"

"Uh, yeah. Sounds pretty bad."

"Disgusting. I don't know who'd do something like this. Maybe a government? Every country is talking war but they don't know who to attack."

"I dunno," said Mark. "I guess they'll figure it out."

Luigi looked at him but stopped himself from saying more. "What'll it be, Mark?"

"I'll have the lasagne with a salad. Can I get some of your black olives with some halloumi cheese to start? Do you still have some bread with seeds? I'll have that. And a Coke."

"Sounds good. I'll bring it over."

"Thanks. Wait, can I get a coffee instead of that Coke? Double black."

"Sure thing, boss." Luigi tore the scribbled page off his pad and handed it to the kitchen behind him. His son Paulo was already preparing the coffee.

The place was busy and someone put the television on to listen to the news. All stations were covering the same event, each showing clips of planes exploding on the ground, presumably taken by those waiting to board other flights. There were no pictures or clips of planes in the air, just debris that fell onto the oceans and deserts and mountains and the heavily inhabited cities and countrysides around the world. It was a catastrophe of biblical proportions. Hundreds of people died on the ground from the falling debris. Thousands more were injured. The trauma caused by this would be hard for everyone to overcome.

"Hope they were insured," someone said. Gallows humour always rose in times of nervous energy.

"My God, who could have done such a thing?" said another.

"*The authorities have suspended all flights worldwide and every nation is on high alert...*" the voice of the newscasters droned on in the background as scenes of devastation and outrage were displayed in still frames and the occasional moving clips. As the hours passed, the news stations would have a deluge of increasingly impressive mini-movies captured by peoples' phones and cameras. "*Talk of war is premature. At this stage, authorities around the world are just trying to understand who could do this type of thing and why.*"

Mark listened to the conversation of the deli patrons and watched the TV out of the corner of his eye, but he came to eat.

He sat down furthest from the entrance door. The shop itself was long and narrow but still wide enough for the deli counter and patrons to fit comfortably near the front with eight tables in the back. The tables could have been at a café in Rome or Milan, set out on the pavement next to the road, attended by glamorous people. Newspapers would be read and cigarettes smoked. Lovers would huddle and exchange kisses and make plans. The tables were round with cane chairs designed to maximise people within a space. Luigi's was set up for people to call ahead and order food and take it home—either for a romantic dinner for two or a sumptuous meal for one. People who ate in the restaurant section were regulars who weren't in a rush and who enjoyed the environment as much as anything else.

Mark enjoyed Luigi's. It was the type of place he would like to own if he could cook. It was like visiting someone's kitchen at home. You would open their fridge and rummage around, pull something out, and then it would be cooked and prepared to your liking. Even better, they made you coffee and had unlimited goodies from the old country, as they called it. There were sweets galore but he tried to keep himself limited to the food.

"Can you believe what's going on, Mark?"

He had to turn to see who was talking. It was another regular. Leanne came from money, people said, and hadn't found her way yet. She received a first class education, travelled the world, and came back home to work in the family business. This allowed her to take long lunches, keep connected to people and, more importantly, reinforce her confidence and lack of fear. She looked at people straight in the eye; her spirit wasn't broken and she retained an optimism about life that inspired friends and kindled begrudging respect from enemies. She was smart and could back up her optimism with real facts and anecdotes. Leanne was one of the first people he met when he was back on his feet. It was also in Luigi's and he was sitting at the table she was now occupying. He liked her energy and enjoyed the time they spent together.

"The world's mad," he said.

"Are you eating alone? Mind if I join you?" She folded her newspaper, pocketed her phone, and bustled over to Mark's table without waiting for an answer. The chair scraped the floor as she moved.

"I don't know much about what's happening," he said. "Sounds like a co-ordinated attack on hundreds of planes. Maybe the government was right and we needed more security. It just seems nuts to me."

"Agreed." Her face was fresh and her hair looked spectacularly natural. Mark knew this meant an expensive regime of hairdressing, possible colouring, and daily management. She wasn't a teenager with the hair of an angel. She was a twenty or thirty something woman of means, comfortable in her skin but unwilling to let go of life's finer things.

"It doesn't look to have been done by any single government because everyone has been affected. What purpose could a terrorist have if they pissed off everyone? Every bad guy needs money and weapons to fight his enemy. Usually you get them from your enemy's enemy."

"Whoever it is will find themselves bombed back to the stone ages when Russia, China, and America get their hands on them. At least this is one thing the three can agree on."

"Funny you say those three countries," she said. "Did you notice you didn't say Europe or any of its countries? France? Germany? England? They are the largest single global economic unit yet they are pygmies on the international stage. They let other countries deal with military security and defence and then complain when America or Russia have too much influence over their policies. Could you imagine Russia outsourcing its security? Unlikely. No one messes with Russia. It's a sclerotic, dying country yet it's a powerhouse militarily and boasts the largest land mass and hoard of natural resources in the world. And no one messes with China. Even America isn't that stupid. Which leads me to wonder whether whoever did this are knuckleheads or farsighted geniuses."

"You really know how to lighten the mood," Mark said with a little grin.

His food started to arrive. She made a motion to leave but he gestured for her to stay. "You eating any-thing?" he said.

"Just finished. I enjoy reading the paper with the background noise and smells of this place."

"I know what you mean. There's something that makes you feel more than just good. You feel safe."

"As long as a plane doesn't fall on us," said Leanne with a smile.

"What happened to you today? Usually you're full of optimism." He broke off a piece of bread and started into his olives and cheese.

"I'm still an optimist but that doesn't change the re-ality around us. We'll survive this and anything else these idiots throw at us. They want us to be afraid and I refuse, but it doesn't mean I can't say that things suck every once in a while." She reached for some bread and popped an olive in her mouth. The bread was fresh and she enjoyed the simplicity of its flavours. She grabbed a black olive and sat back in her chair.

"I couldn't agree more," Mark said. "But this is a big one. I should be afraid but I'm largely indifferent. I guess when it's our time, it's our time. Tolstoy said it nicely in *War and Peace*: 'Every bullet has its billet.'"

"So you believe in fate?" Leanne was helping her-self to some more bread and ate it with the rubbery cheese. Her body was more animated and she leaned in.

"Not fate, but some version of it." He took a piece of the halloumi between his fingers but didn't bite into it. "Take this for instance," he said, gesturing with the cheese. "I came here to eat soft cheese as a starter but I somehow ordered this rubbery stuff. I don't even like it particularly, but I'm here eating it with you. Makes no sense to me. Not sure if that's fate or just pure randomness."

"Well, I like it. Maybe we're supposed to meet here today."

Mark wasn't sure if she was now flirting with him or just being pleasant. He found it difficult to tell at times. He could be charming and others would say he was flirting. He would smile and this would invite conversation. Was this being pleasant and having good manners, or flirting? Most times he was indifferent, his behaviour being a direct result of his blood sugar levels or his general sense of well-being. He knew that many people obsessed about their behaviour or that of other people. He didn't. He tried to be natural and reflect his internal emotions. When he was happy, he would show it on the outside. When he was mad, he would do the same. When he was miserable, he tried to mask it but that, again, was more about manners than anything. Flirting? He didn't know how.

"Maybe," he said. He popped the cheese in his mouth and ate it but didn't grab any more. He focused on the bread and olives. They were fantastic. "What've you been up to lately, other than analysing the geopolitical will of nations and terrorists?"

She smiled. He liked her smile.

"Not much. Same old, same old. Hard not to think about what's going on with the planes. It hurts our family business and will affect every economy in the world. Do you see yourself flying to a tourist destination anytime soon? What'll happen to those places? It'll hurt and the pain will be deep. Sorry, I'm doing it again. I guess everything will change again because of this and we'll need to live a life even more governed by fear and security. My only worry is our loss of freedoms. Soon even conversations like this will be suspected by security forces." She moved some stray hair away from her face and played with the rest for a second.

Mark nodded. "I guess we have to just accept our fate."

"Or some version of it," she said, smiling. Her teeth were perfect and lips full. Only a hint of lipstick remained.

They finished the starters and she watched as the lasagne was placed in front of him. Mark was hungry and started eating straight away after a half-hearted apology. Leanne continued to make light conversation and asked if he was okay with her hanging around with him. It was a long time since he had even been on a date and he was a little afraid of what this entailed, whatever it was. He was just sharing conversation with a woman who frequented the same deli. Perfectly innocent. He tried to put it out of his mind and continued eating.

Leanne kept adjusting herself in her seat, changing her hair from the way it cascaded onto her shoulders to a twisted knot with a spike through it. She talked about the weather, how it was so hot recently, and whether it affected Mark's rehabilitation. She talked about the traffic and how hard it was to find parking in the area. She talked about her work and how she wanted to make her mark with the firm's next building project. She smiled and laughed at Mark's jokes. The tragedy of the day receded and would be dealt with another time.

Mark saw her behaviour and wasn't immune to its effects. He liked her and liked being with her. But why, he thought, did she want to be with him? He was closer to forty than thirty and had a modest means of supporting himself. He wasn't bad looking but he was no movie star, and ten years in a coma hadn't helped his physique. She could do better. She was smart, beautiful, and rich. But he ate his meal and laughed at her jokes and noticed her hand accidently touch his more than once during her explanations. He even joked with her that she could be Italian the way she moved when she talked. That caused her to grab his hands and they both laughed.

"I gotta go," she said with a start. Whether she just noticed the time or she was willing it to go slower was something Mark pondered later. "Look, I'm really glad you let me sit here and spend this time with you." She said this while putting her hand on his forearm. She gathered up her bag, phone, and newspaper and stood up. "I'd really like to do this again sometime."

"Yeah, me too," he said. He found himself standing up.

"Great. It's a date." She pecked him on the cheek and left the shop. She had paid earlier and just waived at Luigi on the way out. As she passed through the door, she turned and looked over her shoulder and smiled at Mark. He waved a little wave and smiled back. Her smile was infectious.

Sitting down to an empty table, he suddenly realised his stupidity. *Why didn't you ask her out, you idiot? You don't even have her number. How're you ever going to meet again? Keep coming here like a lug and hope she'll be here?* He continued to berate himself. His coffee arrived with a small dish of round chocolate balls with icing and a sweet biscuit. *What were you waiting for? Can't you decide what you want? Why can't you do what you want to do?*

It was his first day out on his own without the rehab team since he woke from his coma. There was a global terrorist attack that would alter the daily lives of everyone in the world from that day forward, yet all he could think of was how he could see Leanne again.

By the time he finished his lunch, the world's security services were in overdrive. Talking heads on televisions were predicting anything from hell fire to total social collapse. Radio DJs were playing music and giving commentary that sounded more like your crazy drunk uncle's ramblings. None of it touched on the source or solution to the day's atrocities.

"Getting old Mark? Me too," Luigi said.

"Yeah. I think I was sitting for a bit too long. My body's congealing."

"Could be worse," Luigi said. "You're looking better each time I see you. Have a good day."

"Thanks. You too."

He wanted to walk and keep moving. He heard the voices of the TV as he passed along the corridor in front of the counter towards the door. Catastrophe, brought to you by TV land. Earnest reporters in flak jackets and greying news anchors with their movie star good looks linked the pieces together. The whole world was glued to their news stations and it was the only conversation on anyone's lips.

"Oh, and don't panic about the loss of cell service. The TV said the networks are overloaded. It'll clear eventually."

"Thanks, Luigi. Luckily, I have no one to call."

It was the same during the New York and London attacks over two decades earlier. Wow, twenty-four years since 9/11. It still seemed like yesterday to him. It was already the twenty-fifth of June, 2025. It was moments like this when he felt like Rip Van Winkle.

Since the attacks all those years ago, security had been incrementally stepped up. CCTV cameras created an iron ring around key areas in major cities. Every face and licence was scanned, recorded, and matched against patterns that indicated nogoodnicks. Email and phones were recorded and analysed against similar patterns. Visa and MasterCard expenditures were monitored and profiled. Even Google searches and the ever changing social media forums were monitored and profiled. The reasoning went that you had nothing to fear if you had nothing to hide. Mark wondered how a person could have a private thought, as even that would be self-censored by the person thinking it—just in case it was misconstrued later by the all-seeing eye of security. God may have been dead, according to Nietzsche, but humankind had created something very much in His image: a form of omniscience-induced guilt.

There had, of course, been attacks since those days. Trains, hotels, supermarkets, rock concerts, and even random shooting on the streets. Airports and planes remained a constant target. Sometimes the terrorists were successful. There was outrage, walks of solidarity, and the quiet activities of security services mopping up the stragglers behind the scenes. The population would be told of drone or air strikes killing the perpetrators. Shows of force by the police, military, and politicians were regular events, all designed to reassure the public to go to work, eat out in restaurants, and spend the money necessary to keep the system moving.

Academics, secure in their tenured position, risked nothing, especially not their reputation. They would make pronouncements of the anthropological origins of the conflict and the complex and multi-layered solutions requiring systemic changes in the political machinations of society. These academics vied for television time and recognition as 'the expert' by the networks. It didn't matter to them that their solutions were impractical or impossible. They were there, they said, to balance the argument and to ensure all ideas were aired. Eventually, the public stopped listening.

Mark only read after the fact about the handful of big attacks during his coma. Gassings, mass stabbings, kidnappings. It was hard to know if these were terrorist attacks or just bad people going about their bad business. For that matter, the difference between the two wasn't always clear. What Mark couldn't understand was how certain crimes were on the increase under the nose of this heightened security. Human trafficking, for example, was endemic.

He turned right as he left Luigi's and walked slightly uphill as the road met with the main thoroughfare. There was a massive supermarket there. He didn't recognise the name. It must have taken over the old Safeway store during his coma. There were apartments above the store and other retail shops fronting the pavement. There was a taxi rank with bored drivers waiting for people to come out of the shop or the subway across the road. There was a bank, HSBC, across the road and a church next to that. He could smell the Chinese food shops next to others selling shoes and trendy clothes. *Don't the smells get into the clothes?* he thought.

He smiled and nodded to people he recognised but had never met as they passed each other during his walk. As he approached the park, he passed an ugly building with cages over the windows and a barbed wire fence. There were large garbage bins next to the property, the type that take a special collection truck to lift, but it was otherwise tidy. A sign announced its purpose: The Darcy Sloane Memorial Animal Shelter. He hesitated, pulled back the heavy wrought-iron door, and went in.

Inside, the floors were clean and covered with hospital-style linoleum. The walls were painted white and covered with posters about the well-being and welfare of animals in general but dogs in particular. It could have been a veterinarian's office. There was a smell of disinfectant but it was not unpleasant. There was a young woman behind a desk who smiled at Mark as he entered.

"Hello," she beamed. She couldn't have been more than twenty-five years old and positively glowed with energy.

"Hi," Mark said. "I thought I'd pop in and see what you're all about."

"Are you looking to adopt or just curious?"

"Curious. I need to walk and I was thinking of finding a partner who could join me. This seems like a win-win." He gave a goofy smile. It sounded silly as he said it.

"Perfect." She put her hands on her desk. "We receive a lot of dogs, cats, and even some other more exotic species, but if you are looking for a walking friend, you should look at the dogs." She said she was a dog person but tolerated cats and other animals. Dogs were loyal and reflected their owners. It was one of the reasons why she worked in this place, she explained.

"What are the rules? What do I have to do?" asked Mark.

"It's simple. We get to know you and we have some forms for you to fill in. We then introduce you to our dogs and see which one suits you. You can take him or her for a walk and see how you both gel. If things are still looking good at that point, we just need to ensure that your home is suitable for a dog. This usually means whether you are renting or own your home."

"I own my apartment," Mark said.

"That's good, then there's probably no problem. All we need to do is fill in some paperwork and then go and see who's here."

"Can I look first? I didn't come in here to take home a dog straight away. I was just passing by and the idea struck me."

"Of course. Not a problem. Follow me." She opened the door leading to the kennels in the back and held it open for him.

He could hear the frantic barks of dogs in need of human touch and companionship. Others were silent, looking at him with their heads on their paws, resigned to the inevitable. Some sat stoically and watched him walk past. He could feel they knew why he was there. Orphans looking for homes. Death row mates seeking reprieve.

When he reached the end, he saw a young dog, just older than a puppy but not yet six months' old. It was a light brown colour with its tail chopped short. Its ears hung next to the face. The body was muscular and its face was strong.

"What kind of dog is this?" he asked.

The woman looked at a piece of paper inserted into a groove on the cage. "A South African Boerboel. She's four months old. It's a breed formed from the Mastiff, Great Dane, and St. Bernard by the Dutch and later South Africans to protect farmers from snakes, wild animals, and people. They are powerful and extremely loyal." She stopped and looked at Mark. "You need to be very dedicated to a dog like this. She'll be your best friend but she is also dangerous and could kill someone. This is a big commitment."

"How big will she grow?" Mark said. He was interested in this one. She was beautiful with white paws, freckled with light brown. Her chest was white and the rest of her was a sandy brown. As he looked at her, she didn't bark. She was relaxed and almost docile.

"She is a compact version of this breed. She'll only grow to about 120 pounds, about thirty pounds more than a large Labrador. She's currently at around sixty-five."

"That's a lot of dog," he said. He was wondering whether he could handle her while he was still building up his own walking muscles.

"She'll be what you make her," the woman said. "I've seen a lot of dogs and this one has a wonderful temperament and will be loyal to you to a fault." She smiled. "She's a beautiful specimen, isn't she?"

"Yes. Very striking. You said I could take her for a walk?" He was getting into this.

"Absolutely. Let's get some paperwork done on you and then you can take her to the park and see how you get along."

Mark followed her out and filled in the paperwork. It was an impulsive thing to do but somehow felt right. *Besides*, he thought, *it's just a walk.*

As he opened the door to the fresh air, hand in leash, he reflected on the terrible atrocities of the day and he realised he hadn't thought about it since he opened the door to the shelter. That was a good sign.

Chapter Two

THE REVOLUTIONARY
England,
7 June, 2025

The day was perfect. Blue skies with wisps of clouds and just the slightest breeze. The children would squint as they looked into the sun, then back to their ball game. The grass was freshly cut and gave a clean smell to everything. The brick house stood proud on its ground overlooking the playful children and serious adults. The white marquee stood in stark contrast to its surroundings, beckoning the serious and frivolous alike. The smell of barbeque filled the air. Pork? Some beef? Certainly. An hour or so of speeches and then the crowd could eat and enjoy the glorious day.

"It's my privilege to introduce our guest speaker. He needs no introduction. Please put your hands together for my friend, our leader, the Right Honourable

Fritz Williams." Simon Evans, leader of the local chapter of the conservative party, took a step back and started clapping. The crowd joined in.

They were all volunteers and this was a way for the party to say thank you. They worked tirelessly and faithfully, raising money and corralling opinion sufficient to make this one of the safest conservative seats in the country. Williams, a career politician, wasn't overly fond of these types of gatherings but he tolerated it because they were part of the job. He got elected and ensured the party got elected. This was part of the process, stroking the local volunteer support structure. The grass roots of the party.

Williams shook the hands of the party faithful as he made his way to the front of the marquee. The people loved him and someone stood up, clapping more enthusiastically. Eventually they were all standing and he basked in the unadulterated love. He turned to them and raised his hands in acknowledgement and motioned with those same hands outstretched by a downward motion to have the crowd to sit down.

It was hot inside the marquee and the window sections of the glorified plastic tent were rolled up to expose the undulating green pasture beyond the house's curtilage. Years of experience (primarily disappointment) had taught party planners in England to erect a marquee if holding an outside event. If there was one thing you could be sure of, it was rain.

But not today. Today, the rays of sunshine shone brightly on the marquee and its inhabitants. It shone and made brighter the lush green grass of the surrounding pasture. The long haired highland cattle grazed contentedly. Simon Evans, the local farmer and head of the local conservative chapter, was the host of the event. It was his backyard. The fields surrounding his home, almost as far as the eye could see, were his. He was prosperous and proud of his position, but he also knew that he could not be a politician beyond this village, despite his desire to be on the national stage. He had the wrong body type, the wrong temperament, and the wrong history. He was short and fat like an old Churchill yet he was still young, and he would just get worse as he got older. He told himself this was not good in the age of digital media. He also disliked anyone who disagreed with him, which would be a problem in a system of politics based on arguing. But all of this could have been overcome if it wasn't for the last skeleton in his closet. He had the misfortune of being the descendant of a disgraced Nazi sympathiser. It meant that anytime he would voice an opinion that had even the slightest hint of nationalism—even British nationalism—his Nazi past would be mentioned. He had resigned to being a businessman and promoter of politicians.

The Right Honourable Williams grew up in a privileged position and went to Eton, then Oxford. He was used to the constant changing of clothes during the course of a day for events, sometimes as often as five times. Sports, of course, required a change of clothes, as did lunch, class, and evenings. It was so engrained in him that he didn't think anything of it. Changing was as natural as tying one's shoes. Perhaps this is one of the causes of the English schoolboy's dishevelled look. There was a uniform for each occasion. Today, he would have worn a casual summer cotton suit with an open shirt but for his role as key speaker and guest of honour. Instead, he wore a smart dark blue blazer with shirt and blue tie with a flower in his lapel for some flare. The flower was picked from the garden with the permission of the owner and it made everyone comment at his consideration and uniqueness. It was expected, so he wore it. He held the position of secretary of state in the government's cabinet and had the ear to the most powerful men in the country, not least of whom was the prime minister.

He took his position behind a makeshift podium after shaking Simon's hand. There was no microphone or sound system. The gathering wasn't that big. He was a trained orator and his voice filled the space. The audience sat in rapt attention.

As he spoke, he felt himself blink involuntarily and everything went black. It was as though the lights had been turned off, but the sun was shining. *How could this be?* he thought. He heard noises and felt something bang into his arms and legs. Then it all went quiet. No sun, no noise, no nothing.

The screams were immediate. They were all sitting in rapt attention when Williams' face suddenly bloodied and he crumpled to the floor. On the white plastic marquee behind him was a splattering of what looked like something you blew out your nose, but grey. Lots of it. It was spread out over a foot in diameter.

Williams fell into the adjoining table. His legs banged into the box of wine meant to be raffled after the speech. The front of his face had a hole in it just to the left of the nose, but the back of his head had a hole bigger than a man's fist. He was bleeding and there was no doubt he was dead.

Among the screams and chaos that followed, Simon's mind registered that this was yet another strike against him in his desire to be a national politician.

∞

Jason was breathing no harder than if he had just killed a deer. This was a cull of a different sort. He watched through the scope at the ensuing chaos and slowly got up from his prone position. He had fired off one shot and needed no more. They would work out eventually where the shot came from but by then he would be long gone. He was careful to move slowly, put his rifle into the sling, and disappear into the woods.

This shot was ten years in the making. He had thought of little else and now the time had come. He had stolen the .308 rifle from an owner who wouldn't miss it and would only realise it was gone when the police tracked down and started checking every person who owned one. Jason wasn't foolish enough to be registered anywhere and the ammunition was his own recipe. *It's surprisingly easy to load your own ammo,* he thought. His ammo was loaded to spread violently on impact, causing the exit wound to be massive. It was a hollow point and was illegal in England and most other countries. *Funny,* he thought, *twenty years ago, this would have been the last thing I would have imagined doing.* As he walked through the woods towards his waiting car, he thought about that conversation with Lord Melvin and the unintended consequences that followed.

"Without wealth of their own, the poor have little reason to remain in the system," Jason said.

"You say it as though they have a choice." Lord Melvin dismissed the argument as foolish.

"But the system is crushing them," he said. "They don't have a chance. They are mathematically determined to become serfs—not even peasants, as peasants at least owned their land."

"You're talking nonsense," Lord Melvin said. "There have always been rich and poor. The past, present, and the future are no different."

"But it has gone too far," Jason said. "Democracy itself is at risk. You risk disenfranchising huge swathes of the public just because they're poor."

"I am not doing anything. I'm just a public servant."

"You know what I mean. We need to do something that gives people a chance. We need to redistribute some wealth, or at least seed the ambitions of the less privileged." While the politicians gave lip service to redistribution, no one wanted to donate their own fortunes.

"What do you propose?" The humour was dry. Lord Melvin didn't expect a reply.

"I would do *something*. Look at the housing shortage facing England. Everyone agrees housing is too expensive and that there is a severe shortage of over two million homes but no one wants the new housing in their back yard. Instead, the poor are forced to rent and be shuttled from one crisis to another."

"You can't blame the plight of the poor on NIMBYism," Lord Melvin scoffed.

"True," said Jason. "But it applies to most of capitalism. Those with the capital don't want it disturbed. It will not be given. The government must take it."

"Dangerous words, Jason. I don't think there's the political will for something as dramatic as that."

Jason did try to do something about it and there wasn't the political will for that type of dramatic change. It resulted in him being crushed by the system he was trying to reform. Now he had come up with a new plan for change.

Perhaps it was the result of too many movies or too much time on his hands. While in self-imposed exile, he learned how to shoot from a distance. He joined a gun club in the US and started practicing. He would never be a military quality marksman but he was proficient at six hundred yards and could stretch to a thousand with the right conditions. He realised his new hobby could allow him to carry out his revenge on those who took away his life. At six hundred yards, no level of security could make a man or woman safe at all times. He had no interest in killing someone as powerful as the president of the United States or Russia's dictator *de jour*. Nor did he wish to kill the prime minister. They had done nothing to him, and their security would prevent him from getting close enough, even at six hundred yards. He would be dead shortly after trying. Those were suicide pacts and fantasy. Those particular men and women of supreme political or military power could only be killed by one of their own. Their survival was too important to leave anything to chance.

Lesser cabinet ministers and their families were a different matter. Jason had seen the power of the lone wolf terrorist in the years since 9/11. In his mind, he was no terrorist—more of a freedom fighter or shock-educator—but the concept was the same. A person who had no previous record with the government and who was not on the radar of the security services would not have his phones or emails monitored (even if they were automatically recorded). Jason knew the hype about email and phone surveillance and severely discounted it. They may have recorded his calls and emails, but he was careful in how he accessed the web and used the phone systems. The key was to attack in a random fashion and give lots of time between actions, ideally several months. He must not gloat nor seek glory. Revenge must be served cold and the objective must be only to avenge the wrongs inflicted on him. When this has been achieved, he must stop or else he would have crossed the moral line that separates good from evil.

The killing of Williams felt good. There was no longer any anger or passion, just the resigned determination to carry out what was necessary.

Jason Aldricht was born into an upper middle class family and enjoyed its privileges. His father worked in the City, London's equivalent to Wall Street, and made enough money for his mother to stay at home and take care of Jason and his three brothers. London had seen its fair share of good times and bad. Jason lived during the good times and greatly benefitted as a result.

Following his father's footsteps, he honed his skills earning money working part time jobs and spending time with his father whenever he could. His university studies took him into political studies and economics. He graduated from the London School of Economics with distinction.

He joined a reputable investment bank, which soon merged with one of the top five investment banks in the US. Greed was declared good by the government and soon money was flowing generously.

A keen reader of history, Jason decided to dabble in politics and the power that went with it. He was never a threat to the ruling class and he ensured that he never presented himself as such. He knew when to be deferential and when to appear satisfied with his station in life, but he kept a clear eye on the twin prizes of money and power. He had accumulated the former through his work and within fifteen years had amassed a fortune of over £23 million. He was proud of this. Power was pooling around him as he increasingly had the time and resources to mingle with the super-rich and influential classes of hereditary wealth. Yes, clubs and leisurely past times such as shooting and hunting didn't hurt, but the only way into those inner circles of hereditary and aristocratic wealth was growing up and attending the same schools as them. Even then, you had to be invited into those inner circles; you couldn't earn your way in, and you definitely couldn't force it.

It was 1997 and there was a seismic shift in politics in England as the people shrugged off almost twenty years of conservative rule to hand the reins of power to Labour (or New Labour as they liked to call themselves). Jason saw his opportunity and began to work on a plan to redistribute wealth amongst the people of England, while at the same time adding to his already considerable assets.

"Jason, I know you've been doing well with this business model," his solicitor said.

"So far, so good. Can't complain."

"But people are talking, and I've noticed a number of articles in the paper on you." Mr. Ford took off his glasses, probably for effect. "You are ruffling some feathers."

"I know you have my best interests at heart, but it's a free market. Anyone else is free to do what I do."

"Possibly, but they don't have the guts. Who buys vacant buildings and sells the space in ten square metre sections to foreigners on long leases? It's an asset strip verging on fraud."

"There's no fraud. People can't afford to own their own office in London. I'm making that possible."

"Okay, maybe that model is acceptable, but I've seen what you did to Ozotel Limited. You were hardly helping the little man there."

"Granted," Jason said. "I never said I was a saint. Ozotel was a good old fashioned corporate raid with no survivors. Every last bolt and contract was squeezed out of it. But at least it was finally utilised. It did nothing and would have gone bust anyway."

"But people are complaining that you don't make anything. You don't do anything. All you do is buy up assets and break them apart."

Jason was getting irritated. "Everything I do is legal, and who are these *people* you are talking about? Since when was it distasteful to make money?"

"Since they aren't sharing in the profits. And your most recent venture with land is wholly unappetising."

"What, to sell land to people who otherwise would never be able to afford it? To have a ticket in the game?"

"The powers that be will make you out to be a fraudster."

"Nonsense. I'm not doing anything other than…" He searched for a word to describe it. "Democratising land ownership." He smiled at his own invention.

"Be careful. There's no appetite for this type of thing in the UK. You should know better than to poke the lion."

Initially this didn't cause any difficulties, but as luck would have it, Jason did one of his asset strip operations (his solicitor called it the 'slice and dice') next to a small town that boasted the mistress of a prince and a mistress to the then acting secretary of state. The mistress of the prince knew better than to abuse her access and was quiet. The other one was not schooled in the same manner and wished for her outrages to be visited upon the egregious developer. At the time, Jason had no idea he had offended anyone (other than the normal jealousy success breeds), nor that there was such a back-channel of power still in existence in England.

As Jason would learn the hard way, it was still firmly entrenched.

It started in 2007 and continued until 2013. First came the enquiries from government departments associated with the secretary of state like the Department of Trade and Industry. Then came the tax audit on him and all his companies. Then came the 'investigative journalism'. He survived each line of attack. In fact, the

UK tax office owed *him* millions of pounds due to an accounting quirk. He settled the dispute by agreeing that they didn't owe him anything provided both parties walked away and the audit was vacated. Being pragmatic, Jason felt it was important to eliminate enemies and fights he couldn't win. While he had the upper hand on that point, the tax office had both unlimited resources and the power to grind him down. At the time of the settlement, they had already been working on the file for four years. It was a war of attrition and no individual could win such a battle against a state.

Negative articles in the paper inspired clients to turn on him and sue for perceived damages. Class action lawsuits started raining down. Cash flow dried up and reversed as money was diverted into his defence. His business was all but shut down. It was gradual, like a string of bad luck that wouldn't cease.

Even that, Jason took in stride. *We're all big boys here*, he thought. *It may get a little rough and tumble, but that's why some people are bosses and the rest are employees.*

Then came the nail in the coffin. Not being able to shut him down legally, the secretary of state took out the nuclear option. Jason received the petition to wind up his businesses on public interest grounds.

"Are you sure they can do that?" Jason asked.

"They have virtually unlimited power and they win 98% of these cases. You may win, but the odds are long against you." Ford was solemn.

"Can we fight?"

"You have to fight. We'll do this for you but there's no future for you here."

"What about the companies? What'll happen to me?"

"All of the bank accounts will be frozen. We'll try to unfreeze things and allow you to wind down operations in an orderly manner while we fight the petition. Depending on how things go, they may reverse all of the dividends you have paid yourself over the years. They will then go after you personally to reimburse the company for them."

Jason was dumbstruck. "How is this even possible? How far back?"

"Back to year dot." Ford was cautious not to enflame Jason any more than he needed to, but he had to set out the worst case scenario.

"You mean they'll take everything I have and everything I had? Those dividends weren't illegal. I had a top three accounting firm do my books. Doesn't that count for anything?"

"I'm just setting out a worst case scenario. We'll do our best to make sure that doesn't happen."

Jason slumped down heavily. He had already been sitting. It seemed as though he shrunk with the news. "Okay. Bad stuff. It's bullshit, but what can I do?"

"Do you have some money tucked away?"

"Some. Not a lot. I put everything into these businesses. If they take that, I'll be practically penniless."

"Do the companies have any money in them?"

"Sure. Lots of cash, lots of assets. But when the creditors find out, they'll eat me alive."

"I know. It's a difficult process."

"What would you do?"

"I'd make sure I had some money and go for a holiday. Leave it to us to fight for you. Be available by phone and email. Try to take up a hobby."

This is what Jason did. His hobby, unfortunately for Fritz Williams, was long range target practice.

Jason gathered what money he had outside of the businesses and decided to leave England. All monies in his businesses were frozen until the outcome of the petition. He would fight and vowed to throw everything he had at the secretary of state. Every delay, every trick, every possible way to increase costs to the government and improve his position of victory was employed. Instructions were set and he left the UK.

That was 2015 and he lived his self-imposed exile for almost ten years while he waited for all actions, investigations, and assaults against him to cease. During his exile, his primary concern was the safety and liquidity of his capital. He knew if he failed, the long arm of the law would hunt down his life savings and gobble them up without so much as a burp. Any business he started would be strangled, uprooted, and liquidated on the appointed date.

He waited until the dust settled and he could hit back. *If they were going to cheat in stopping him, he would have to cheat as well*, he told himself. The number of rules and regulations enacted by politicians in the UK and around the world seem to be aimed at criminalising the population. It was as though the pencil pushers had taken over the government. Every action and inaction was codified and made legal or illegal. *What these legislators forget,* he told himself, *is that people don't think like that. People are mostly good.* He believed this, but even good people do stupid things from time to time. If the net that held society together was too tight, it would strangle the good and bad alike. The result would be revolution.

Well, Jason thought, *I've been pushed long enough. Now it's my turn to push back.* He wanted to avenge the injustice visited upon him. What others did was their business. Any animal, when cornered, will turn to fight. He had stopped running, stopped cowering, and was ready to strike back.

It was coincidence that the time he chose to launch his battle was just two and a half weeks before the synchronised global terrorist attack. After it happened, he convinced himself that his actions were part of a general movement of discontent by the people against their governments. He was part of some larger movement. *There is a wind of change in the air*, he thought. *It is a summer of global discontent.*

∞

11 June, 2025

"Did you hear about Fritz Williams?"

"Dreadful. Truly dreadful."

Mrs. Beau put her umbrella in the stand near the door. She was around sixty and was known to everyone as the town gossip. If you wanted the world to know something, you would tell her.

"I'm just so glad my Harry is out of the game," Jennifer Collins said in reply. It was widely known that she was the girlfriend of Harry Constable at the time he was secretary of state, around fifteen years prior. She was still pretty and wore her dresses short and tight. Luckily, she still had the body for that. Sir Harry still saw her but much less frequently. He preferred his girls of a certain age and mind set. While Jennifer's mind didn't alter, her body couldn't defy time. She was now forty-two and past her sell-by date, as she said to her friends.

"Have they discovered who did it or why?" Mrs. Beau asked. She started walking into the lounge towards the liquor cabinet. She enjoyed her alcohol.

"How would I know?" said Jennifer. "I'm no longer privy to anything. I'm just a washed up old has-been." She allowed herself to start feeling sorry for herself and accepted a large gin and tonic from her friend.

"Ah, men," Beau said. "They can't have enough of you, will bend over backwards for you, and go to war for you. Anything. Just don't grow old. Even I was known to turn a head or two in my day. Now, they look the other direction."

"Not true," Jennifer said. "I know for a fact that John down the lane is sweet on you."

"Ah, shut up. He's sweet on Jamieson's sheep too." Beau said it straight faced but couldn't keep up the act. She started laughing. Jennifer joined in.

"The police are treating it as a terrorist attack. They've increased security and are taking no chances. Not one clue." She couldn't stop thinking about it. What if Harry was shot? She couldn't bear it.

"I'm sure they'll find whoever is behind it. Some malcontent or pissed off banker. Who knows why someone does something like that?" Beau felt her liquor quickly. Her tongue loosened. She rarely held back at the best of times and the booze released whatever inhibitions she may have had.

"Don't be monstrous, Pam," Jennifer said. Beau didn't like begin called by her first name. Pamela sounded like an American stripper, she said. "What do they have to gain from killing poor old Williams? He's only doing his job. He's done nothing wrong."

"Who knows what goes on in the minds of madmen," Beau continued. "All someone needs to do is to think that violence will solve the solution and *voilà*, the violence begins."

Jennifer agreed. Sometimes Beau made sense.

"If your wife is out of line, just knock some sense into her," Beau continued. "If someone steals a loaf of bread, put him in chains. Better yet, hang him. Maybe that'll keep the crime down."

"I know you're joking, but how do we stop a person like this?"

"Let him keep killing. It wouldn't hurt to kill the odd politician." Beau had downed her first two drinks and was on number three.

"You are behaving terribly today," Jennifer scolded with a half-smile. "Have you had anything to eat yet?"

"No, why?" Beau looked at Jennifer. She liked her morning drinks.

"Have a seat and I'll fix us some scones with cream and jam. I know you like it. I could use a little something in me too."

Beau found a comfortable chair. She was feeling just fine and wasn't sure what Jen was talking about. She looked out the window of the lounge onto the undulating hills of the Kent countryside. "It must be wonderful to have a view like this, without any neighbours overlooking you," she said to herself as much as Jen.

"What?" came Jen's voice from around the corner in the kitchen.

"Nothing, dear."

"What? I can't hear you. Just a minute, everything is prepared. I'll be right out."

Jennifer came out with a flowered bone china tea service on a plastic flowered tray. The Minton tea pot and cups with matching saucers were a present from Harry. He had certain standards and drinking tea from English bone china was one of them. It just made the tea taste better, he said. Next to the tea set were the scones, bought from the local bakery but tasty, and dollops of clotted cream and strawberry jam.

"Very civilised," Beau said and clapped her hands in appreciation. She finished off her drink and put it aside.

Jennifer walked the tray into the conservatory overlooking the open countryside. She liked to call it an orangery but it wasn't large enough and her house wasn't grand enough to pull it off. Besides, the only fruit growing in this conservatory were her guests.

The glass room was spacious and provided the perfect airy space in which to enjoy a spot of tea. The table and chairs were set up for entertaining and there were soft furnishings next to the walls where people could flop—in a civilised manner, naturally. In the middle of the room was a round table with its wings, as she called them, folded. The result was a rectangular table suitable for two to sit and have tea. Their chairs were not overly comfortable as they were made from wrought iron. They had little cushions on the seats to make them bearable.

Beau had not left her seat in the lounge and was looking towards Jennifer. She watched as the place settings were laid and everything was made perfect. Then her friend turned towards her and beckoned her to join her. The light of the outside created an aura around Jennifer. Beau would later say it was as though she was an angel.

At that moment, Beau saw and heard two things that changed her life forever. One was the disappearance of Jen's face and the other was the sound of glass breaking. Or was it the other way around? The shot had entered Jen's head from the back. As a result of the glass slowing down the bullet, it began expanding too early. When it hit Jennifer, it tore holes in her, causing the lead to tumble and create even bigger holes out the front of her head.

Beau still had her smile on her face as she watched her good friend fall down dead in front of her. She was still sitting in her chair in the lounge. Her body jolted from the horrific disjunction of the expected and new reality. She had expected to glide from the lounge chair into the conservatory and enjoy some scones with cream and jam. Instead, her body was filled with adrenaline. She became cold and sober, and shit herself.

∞

Jason collected the shell casing from the chamber and put his rifle into the sling. He got in the car he had 'borrowed' for the day, careful to make no mess. His shoes had plastic covers on them, similar to hair nets you might see a cook wearing at McDonalds. They gave the added benefit of reducing clues for the police. No treads.

Jason had been worried about this shot. Shooting through glass with the sun's glare meant a real chance that he would fail. But he was determined to take only one shot and if he missed, he would still leave. Death was not the primary objective. Discipline, apparent randomness, and patience. That was the key to his plan, and it would be realised soon enough by the powers that be. These initial murders were the educational tools he would bequeath to the people of the world, for this was not just about the UK but the way in which politics, power, and money had evolved in the West.

A forest fire, large or small, starts with the same spark. If a young man shot dead by police could start riots throughout London, Manchester, and Birmingham, as they did in the not too distant past, then the roadmap of how to unseat those in power and reinstate a more democratic rule of law in Britain was possible. All the people needed was a way to achieve it. It would be a revolution, a small civil war, and then reinstatement of a new status quo. It was a call to arms by those who had lost faith in the ballot box and the disconnected rulers who presided over them.

Jason was careful not to travel on the M25, the perimeter highway of London, nor on any motorways leading into the city. They had been outfitted with facial and licence recognition software and were all fed into a super computer that cross checked and looked for patterns. This was a powerful tool in the hands of the police. The cameras were not all about controlling traffic; they were about controlling people.

He drove the back roads and found his parked car. He lit his getaway car on fire the way youngsters did after a joy ride and disappeared into the background noise of the mundane. Just another day. Just another bloke going from point A to point B.

∞

"My dear boy, they must have issued a D-Notice. There's no way two bodies could have been pulled from a lake next to Sevenoaks without so much as a murmur unless the press was instructed not to report it." Oliver was into his third pint and was lecturing Jason and Colin about the dark arts of the press and national security.

"Naturally, we used this widely during the Irish terrorist attacks to take the wind out of the publicity they would have otherwise generated." Oliver was ex-Special Forces SAS and had spent his fair share of time in Belfast. He was also half Irish.

Jason remembered this conversation and found it odd that even the foreign press had not reported on this. He guessed the anti-terrorist sections of MI5 had managed to get there before anyone else could be notified, but the other person in the room must have called 999. There was no way the police could get there before the ambulance. Even if they did, how did they keep everyone quiet?

For Jason, it was confirmation of the power the government had over the people without them even knowing it.

∞

Jason's home was a modest-looking detached three bedroom house on the outskirts of a nameless town in

Surry. He had some privacy, around seven acres, with a garage and gate that blocked prying eyes. The drive was curved and full of rhododendrons, their evergreen leaves shielding the house from the road.

"Remember to take all of your filings and spare bits of metal and create a conspicuous mess. You want to hide things in plain sight. Deep beneath this pile of metal filings you can bury your guns and ammo, but preferably in a place even harder to reach." The survival video tape was surreal to Jason at first but its lessons stuck with him. "But holes and diversions will only take you so far," the narrator droned on. "Your true enemy is yourself. Your own big mouth. Keep it shut and your chances of betrayal drop considerably." Jason's paranoia extended to his computer searches. He ensured that he didn't visit any site he wouldn't be happy for his mother to know about.

In his toilet hung old reminders from the world wars, like "Loose lips sink ships" with pictures of a soldier talking to a beautiful woman, and "The walls have ears" with pictures of soldiers in a pub laughing too loudly and a person in the adjoining booth leaning over with interest. Silence is the greatest weapon of the revolutionary. The Irish were famous for it. The Arabs and the Muslim extremists are more successful because of it. As he drove up his driveway, his mind recalled an earlier conversation with his drinking mates.

"What do those bastards in Whitehall do? They start eavesdropping on the good guys. Us. Interfering with our private lives." Colin and Oliver were well into their cups.

Jason joined in. "I never understood why the government didn't take a simpler approach to terrorism and murder. They should arrest anyone associated with the crime and prosecute them to the full extent of the law. If you help a murderer through silence, you become an accessory to murder. Likewise with terrorism. Why didn't the government take this position?"

"Because we don't have the manpower," Oliver said. "We like to fool our people into thinking that we know everything and see everything but we don't. We pick our fights for maximum impact. Lately, it has all been about intelligence gathering with minimal disruption to the public."

"Power perceived is power achieved," said Jason.

"Exactly," said Colin. "When disruptive people arrive on the scene and challenge that power, the government becomes fearful of what such an individual can inspire in the public. Think about Michael Collins of Ireland, Ghandi of India, and Bin Laden of Saudi Arabia. They demonstrated the power of poking the government in the eye. Backed by the people, Michael Collins created a revolution that eventually saw the British out of Ireland; Ghandi led a peaceful revolution against the British in India; and Bin Laden demonstrated that America was not invulnerable, leading to widespread war and disruption of governments across the Muslim and Arab world."

As Jason took another mouthful of his beer, he marvelled at how well his drinking mates held their liquor. Barely a slur and still articulate. The beer loosened their tongues but didn't affect the delivery of message.

"Dear boy, I wouldn't go so far with your Irish point, but I do agree with the others. Shame about India. I did enjoy my stay there." Oliver must have been into his fifth pint.

For Jason, it was also clear that to go down this path meant a near certain early death. But death would have to wait for dinner at his parents. He washed, burned his clothes, and made his way to London by train. His brothers would be there and he always enjoyed the banter of a family dinner.

∞

"Have you heard about this crazy killer?" Tom asked with his mouth full of vegies while reaching for his wine.

"What?" Jason asked. He felt a burning in the pit of his stomach.

"This crazy killer in the States," continued James, Jason's other brother. "Just went into his high school and shot his teacher and principal dead where they stood. They didn't even know what was happening. The kid was seventeen and loaded to the teeth. By the time they stopped him, he'd killed seven teachers, the principal, and fifteen girls. He was eventually killed by the SWAT team. What a lunatic. Apparently, none of the girls liked him because he was fat and had terrible acne. He probably also smelled like a sewer and farted when no one was looking." James couldn't help but add his commentary to the tragedy.

"What do you think he was trying to achieve?" Jason's mother asked. "It's just killing for no reason, and we'll never know for certain what his hang ups were. Sounds like a troubled child. I feel sorry for him."

Tom finished chewing and added, "But nothing as cool as the Washington sniper who kept shooting people from the boot of his car while his son drove. Shut down the entire state." He smiled.

"That's equally disgusting," their mother said. "It's cowardly, especially killing innocents. He's worse than that kid in the high school. He should've known better."

Guess I shouldn't tell them about my latest hobby, thought Jason. He grabbed a bread roll, poured himself some wine, and enjoyed the meal. He didn't contribute to the conversation much.

∞

16 June, 2025

The video on the internet appeared to be from the perspective of a scope. The cross-hairs were visible and the field of view was round.

When Chief Superintendent Judd first saw the video after being notified by a concerned citizen, he felt his bowels liquefy. He saw the viewpoint and crosshairs scan the horizon with its imposing brick house, children playing, and white marquee. The voyeur was patient as he (presumably it was a he) focussed. Then the view was magnified and the people in the marquee were visible. The busybodies making everything right, the patrons and volunteers shuffling into position and making polite conversation. Eventually the then secretary of state came into view. The viewer didn't flinch or make any changes. The viewpoint was sharpened into a tight focus and there was a jiggle as a hand must have touched the scope to do so.

"Do I need to watch all of this shit?" Judd turned to the other people in the room.

"Sir, I think you should see this." A young attendant was transfixed by the macabre killer's view.

"Have forensics come up with anything?" Judd asked.

"Just received this. They're analysing as we speak." The attendant answered but didn't break his stare. This was the first time any of them were watching it.

"Damn the internet," mumbled Judd. "Is there any way we can get this removed?"

"Our guys are working on it," said Sergeant Moxxit. "My understanding is that once this is out of our jurisdiction, we can't request or enforce a security ban."

"We're getting reports of this video from China and the middle east. Al Jazeera is broadcasting it unedited over its entire network." Doug Mort was the IT guy and was watching and monitoring his laptop while talking.

After Williams' assassination, the video changed to Collins' killing. It showed the patience of the killer as the victim was clearly available to be shot many times before the fatal hit.

"What's he waiting for?" Judd said. "Why shoot her in the back of the head through glass? Why not shoot her as she came out of the car or when she lingered outside?"

No one spoke for a while.

"Sir, maybe he wanted it to be as messy as possible," the unnamed attendant said. "It almost looks personal, as if he wanted her face to be blown off."

"You're aware of this killing?" Judd asked the man.

Everyone nodded. This was the task force assembled when Jennifer Collins was killed. The computer caught the connection, however tenuous, and alerted the need to investigate.

Chief Superintendent Barry Judd was sixty-four and had been heavily involved with the IRA troubles in Ireland and then England. He was trained in the elite SAS and was recruited by MI5 once the more physically demanding elements of his SAS duty were behind him. Age prevented him from being on the front line any longer. His body had taken enough punishment— broken bones, torn muscle and flesh, shot twice, and stabbed five times. MI5, the UK's security services, were impressed with his work in Lebanon and Libya as well as Ireland. They valued discretion. Judd would be their man.

The Joint Terrorism Analysis Centre used its influence within the Metropolitan Police Service of Greater London to ensure that Judd would be high enough to be effective and still have value to MI5. It was a blurring of the lines that wasn't publicly known or condoned. But MI5 was all about the survival of the UK against all threats domestic and foreign. Judd was within the Specialist Operations of the Met in charge of counter terrorism. SO15 had called this meeting and Judd was chairing.

"Sir, the next killing is the third and last."

The video continued as the scenes of a golf course came into view. Judd took a quick intake of breath when he saw the prime minister next to the third victim, playing golf. It was the sixth green at the famous St. Andrews golf course, not far from Edinburgh. The now familiar round view scanned the horizon, stopping to identify the plain clothes security officer before continuing on.

"The bastard wants us to know he knew where our security detail was," Judd fumed. He was starting to dislike this killer. Too dangerous by half.

Then the familiar shake as the scope moved with the recoil of the shot. It then searched and found the dead body of Lord Staines lying in a heap immediately next to the prime minister, who looked surprised and was then surrounded by his security and bundled off the course.

When the video ended, Judd erupted. "Why the blazes did he shoot Staines and not the PM?"

"Sir, maybe he missed?" offered Moxxit.

"This guy didn't miss," Judd said. "He wanted Staines dead. But why? And what the fuck is the connection between these poor souls?"

"Sir, there's more." The attendant motioned to the screen.

Patience. One shot. 300-600 yards. Kill only the cause of our corruption. Embrace the Revolution. The words appeared and stayed long enough for even slow readers to catch them.

"Now we have a fucking revolutionary on our hands?" Judd's swearing increased the angrier he got. "Who the fuck does he think he is? Che fucking Guevara?"

"Sir, the PM is looking for a report," said Mort. It was being demanded by the Cabinet Office Briefing Room. The press and most everyone simply called it COBRA.

"Of course they want a fucking report! These people are dead. His secretary of state, a mistress of a former secretary of state, and the PM's fucking biggest contributor are dead. He's probably the biggest contributor to the conservative party, for Christ's sake. We need to find out who the fuck did this and stop a public fucking panic before it's too fucking late!"

"Sir?"

Judd reeled around to look at the attendant, his eyes bulging and the vein in his neck taught as a rope. "What the fuck now?"

"There's more. There's a new video that just came on line."

"Have our experts tracked the fucking IP address? Find this fucker and bring him to me." Judd was getting pissed. He tried to calm himself down and added, "Okay, now, what's this new video all about?" It would have been comical if the situation wasn't so serious. Judd kept his emotion in check and watched the next video. It was much shorter, but its message hit him in the gut. There was no sound initially. Just words. Then a computer generated voice started reading the slowly scrolling script. It said eerily:

This is a call for a revolution!

Let's make the lives of our children better than ours.

Right now, we're living a lie. There's no pie for you or me. It's hoarded by the rich and powerful and they refuse to share.

"Who is this fucker? A fucking baker or a fucking revolutionary?" fumed Judd aloud.

And this will continue until a real change takes place.

The solution is political. But the electorate needs a leader. There is no will within the current leadership.

I am here to tell you there IS *a solution, but its implementation will require the re-education of the political, financial, and ruling classes.*

They will resist so we must insist.

Victory means each of you to do just one thing: remove the most powerful man or woman around you.

Just one shot.

Don't be a hero. Keep it random and have no connection to yourself.

Do not avenge a perceived injustice against yourself. Attack the head of the corrupt beast and the body shall fall.

One person, one shot, one kill.

And we will win.

After that, it scrolled back to the beginning. The eerie voice droned on.

"Fuck!" Judd said and slammed the door behind him.

Chapter Three

THE TEENAGERS
Israel,
25 June, 2025

Gabriel was making some carrot juice to clear out the fridge. He bought an entire carton of carrots and needed to get rid of them before they started to go bad. In times like this, he would make a full litre of juice. It took thirty large carrots and he drank it all himself. He was told he could get carrot poisoning and his skin would turn orange but he dismissed this as nonsense.

His juicer was a basic unit and did what he needed. It wasn't loud but he had to turn up the radio to drown out the motor. As he finished, he put the juice on the kitchen table alongside a glass and a baked potato from yesterday evening. It wasn't gourmet but it was nutritious. The radio was blaring and he heard a noise that made him stop in his tracks. It was a distant wailing.

He knew that sound. He waited to see if it was just a large truck going through its first and second gears but realised it was what he feared most.

He turned off the radio and the sound continued. It wailed. Within seconds, it was joined by a second one, closer. Louder. Then a third and fourth and fifth erupted, each increasingly urgent. His adrenaline started pumping. This wasn't a test. These were air raid sirens used to indicate incoming missiles. His body became calm and waited for the iron dome defence system; the incoming missiles would be exploded by rockets shot upwards. To him, it was like a miracle when it worked and Tel Aviv survived its fair share of missile attacks. In 2014 alone, over four thousand missiles were shot into Israel from Gaza, he recalled.

This time, there were no explosions from the iron dome. Instead, pieces of debris from a plane crashed into Tel Aviv. The streets exploded with sirens as the infrastructure of defence secured the city and dealt with injuries. Israel was a country born after the most destructive global conflict and existed in a state of constant war since 1948. This was just another page in its history.

"What's going on, Abba?" His son ran to him.

"Get your mother and sister and get everyone into the Miklat." Gabriel hated that his children needed to be rushed into bomb shelters and safe spaces so often. The Miklat, or Mamad, was the safe place in an apartment and was required by Israeli law. Gabriel set up his home office in the family Miklat. He would move the family to the larger bomb shelter if required. He needed to hear the news and find out what happened and what was happening.

During the event, Gabriel was calm. It was after, when the tears would swell, that the anger would return. *What good does all this killing achieve?* The sounds brought him back to 2014 and day he met his wife to be. He was seventeen years old, cocky, and in love.

∞

Tel Aviv, summer, 2014

"Let's go!" Imbal yelled over the buzzing of their Vespa scooters' engines. She had a helmet on, pink with swirly designs. She was slim and all Gabriel could see was her long legs with her sandals. Her shorts were cut off jeans, cut so high that a little bit of her bum showed. It was the fashion, and who was he to argue with it?

"I'll race you. Loser pays!" Gabriel revved his scooter as though it was a big rumbling Harley. His helmet was black with speckles, like the sky with stars. They were off to the beach to find a food stand famous for its falafels. It was frequented by truck drivers, teachers, and politicians but was inundated by young adults. It was cheap, healthy, and fast.

The high pitched whine of their scooters was a familiar sound throughout Israel and, in fact, throughout most of the Mediterranean. Scooters were cheap to buy, easy to fix, and easier to ride. If you could ride a bicycle, you could ride a scooter. Gabriel and Imbal's were just over a year old. They had each received one for their sixteenth birthdays.

As they were dodging stationary traffic and the occasional person crossing the road, Imbal screamed and started swerving wildly. She veered off the road, slamming heavily into the blue painted curb. She was thrown from her scooter and landed only inches from some stray cats, which scattered in double time. Gabriel saw this, pulled over, and ran to her. There were already two women crouched over her and a handful of fascinated children looking on.

Imbal was not stationary. She was screaming and kicking her legs. Her arms were frantically trying to remove her helmet. The two women were trying to calm her. The more they told her to be calm, the more she screamed. Gabriel arrived just as the helmet came off. She was wildly shaking her hair and using her hands to clean something off her face and hair.

"Imbal!" Gabriel cried. "Imbal, I'm here. You're okay."

"Gabe," she said, "I'm okay. Just an accident." The heavy breathing and frantic look quickly subsided. She smiled and thanked the two women who stopped. The children were theirs and they were just getting some ice cream before heading to the beach. The women lingered briefly to ensure everything was okay and then carried on.

"What happened?" Gabe had his palm lightly on her back. *She's not wearing a bra*, he thought, then chided himself for the inappropriateness of this thought.

Imbal leaned into him and put an arm around him in a half hug. "Must have been a bee or something. It hit my eyeball and then somehow got into my helmet. I felt it fly into my ear. That's when I veered off the road."

Gabe wrapped both his arms around her. She was slim and athletic, her muscles supple. He was initially frightened by her accident but now was incredibly drawn to her, partly to protect her but mostly by his desire to have sex. At that age, that was all he thought about.

"You were amazing," he said instead of acting on his impulse. "I don't know what I would've done if something like that happened to me."

Imbal moved away slightly but still held his fingers. "Thanks." They stood silent for a couple of seconds but Gabe would remember that time for the rest of his life. They looked at each other and both knew.

"Still up for the beach?" she said and started towards her fallen chariot. Surprisingly, it was undamaged. The shield on the front that protected the legs was cracked but otherwise it seemed to be okay. "I'll get my brother to look at it for me later," she said with a shrug. She carefully steered it back onto the edge of the road and picked up her helmet. This time she secured it to the back seat with a little bungee cord. She may be getting back in the saddle but wasn't yet prepared to put on the cage that captured her tormenting bee.

"Absolutely. Are you sure you're okay?" Gabe's concern was sincere, but he was also looking forward to seeing Imbal in her bikini. He wondered at times what she was doing with a guy like him. He was athletic but plain. He wasn't the captain of any team but he played all the sports. He enjoyed beach volleyball and liked surfing the Tel Aviv waves when the winds were right. His family wasn't rich and he wasn't the smartest guy in school. She, on the other hand, was a stunning twelve out of ten. Her lithe body had the confidence of a fighter pilot and it showed in her walk, talk, and general attitude to life. She was tough but all woman. Her family was well off and she was possibly the smartest girl in school.

"Yeah. Just a little shaken up. Still hungry?"

They both smiled, hopped on their scooters, and buzzed away into traffic. Next stop, falafel and shawarma.

Poems are written, songs are sung, and neither can capture the power of your lover's hand holding yours. That simple act, hand in hand, two figures walking, forms the cornerstone of all humankind. That day at the beach, her hand in his, bound them as if wed.

"Have you thought about where you'll serve?" The question was innocent. Imbal didn't want this moment to end. She felt that jolt when he held her after her crash. She saw him jolted as well.

"Not that we have much of an option," Gabe said. "We'll be evaluated and slotted into whatever area they think is best."

"We can ask," she said.

"Sure, you can ask. I can ask for peace but that doesn't mean we'll get it." Gabe swung his leg out to catch the water, creating a bigger spray.

"Then let's not worry about it until then." She stopped walking, turned to Gabe, and kissed him. It was their first kiss. She leaned in slowly, turning her head up slightly and let Gabe close the distance. Gabe felt a surge of adrenaline shoot to every extremity in his body. He tasted her saltiness amidst the sweat and spray. She reached up and tenderly touched his face, never letting her lips leave his. His hands went up tentatively to her waist. His body was going into sensory overload.

When they pulled away, their eyes were locked on each other and a smile began to form on each other's mouths. It was morning and the beach was full of the usual suspects. She allowed her eyes to glance down quickly and back to his. She smiled more fully. He shrugged his shoulders and put on a goofy grin. In response, she grabbed his hand and pulled him into the water. They fell into the surf laughing, she in pure enjoyment, and he in pure relief.

When the first air raid siren in Tel Aviv sounded, Imbal and Gabe were in bed, spent. Her parents were away on business and the two took advantage of the situation. It was Gabe's first time. It was Imbal's first time in love. It was a surreal moment, both of them fully relaxed, hormones coursing through their naked bodies beneath a cotton sheet. The sound of the air conditioning was so constant it didn't register to their senses, but the wailing was new. Then another siren sounded, closer. Then another.

The explosions began. They ran to the apartment's safe room and vowed they would dash for the basement's more secure bomb shelter next time. Windows rattled, cutlery clinked, and they felt the percussive sound of large ballistics. This was not a drill. They were under attack.

Not that they didn't know it was coming. The news was full of the impending conflict with Gaza. "I didn't think they would do it," Imbal said. Her eyes were wide and she clutched her iPhone. She posted a message on Facebook saying she was safe. Gabe did the same. They both huddled over the phone and monitored the events as they unfolded.

"I noticed the streets were empty," Gabe said. "But they've been that way for over two weeks. Why today?"

"Because today they were ready," Imbal replied. "I've heard my cousins talking. This time it could be really bad." She shook slightly.

Another set of explosions rattled the windows. The sirens continued to wail.

"I wouldn't want to be in Gaza today," joked Gabe. "We're going to kick their asses back to the Stone Age."

"They're already in the Stone Age," Imbal said. She wasn't joking. She was grim. She knew people would be dying on both sides of this fight.

"I wonder if the iron dome will hold?" Gabe said. "I've seen the tests on You Tube but it does seem amazing."

"Amazing," Imbal repeated.

Another three explosions. Moments later, the sirens fell silent.

Gabe was holding Imbal's hand and the two were silent, shaking a little from the adrenaline and the novelty, both putting on a brave face for the other. They knew if the missiles actually hit Tel Aviv, the army's response would be a hundred times worse than if they were intercepted by the dome. It was a system of rockets shot from the ground at the incoming missile. The ground rockets would explode near the incoming rocket, making it harmless. Generally, two missiles were shot from the ground for every one incoming. For the citizens of Tel Aviv, it was a miracle, and at

$20,000 a shot, it was a profitable business for someone.

The phone rang and they both jumped. "Mom? Yeah, I'm okay. I love you too. No, not a problem. Everything is fine. Everything's safe. The army went in this morning." She was speaking a mile a minute, responding before questions were asked, relieved at the call. "When are you coming home? Great, I can't wait to see you. Love to Dad. Bye…" Her voice trailed off as she pulled the phone from her ear. She turned to Gabe and he pulled her next to her. They both had tears in their eyes.

∞

When they finished high school, they joined the army. It was compulsory; no one liked it but, as everyone did it, it was accepted. He was assigned to the paratroopers, she to intelligence. The experience scarred Gabriel deeply but hardened Imbal. She was still herself, but seeing and knowing the evils of the world made her examine options that were unthinkable even two years before.

"Don't you think it's a good idea?"

"Sure," Gabriel said. "But it's dangerous and you could get hurt."

"But if we all did nothing we'll get hurt anyway." Imbal wasn't budging.

"America will protect us. Why put yourself in harm's way?"

She snorted. "America will do what's right for America. We are no longer the toe hold for them in the Middle East. If you haven't already noticed, they have washed over us. They are moving their front line as far east as possible. Just look at where their military bases are."

"Why?" Gabe wasn't that interested but Imbal agreed to marry him and he wanted children. He humoured her but didn't want to see her hurt.

"The Middle East is a distraction for the world. It's not a prize. It has strategic value in terms of shipping routes and oil. Now it also has the added value of being close to the next big conflict when the big boys start fighting."

"Big boys?"

"When the real powers of the world butt heads. Russia, China, America. But soon this will include India. It's being armed in anticipation."

"Anticipation for what?"

"China, Russia, anyone. Take your pick. America doesn't want to see its largest natural ally and the only real democracy in that part of the world fall into enemy hands."

"And this is important to us how?"

"Gabe, sometimes I don't think you listen to me." She play-punched him and smiled. They had both just finished their army service and were enrolled at Technion University, partly because it was Israel's answer to MIT but also because it was based in Haifa and they could share a flat rather than stay at home like they would if they went to the Tel Aviv University. "There is a real opportunity for us. India is arming and we can be part of it."

"Okay, but how? There are people who are doing this already. Why would they buy from us?"

"There are a million burger and falafel and coffee shops but people open new ones every day. We just need to be clever."

Gabriel wondered where Imbal got this drive from. They grew up in the same neighbourhood, went to same school, and had the same friends. Sure, her family had more money than his, but otherwise they had almost an identical upbringing. And yet she was head and shoulders above him when it came to this type of stuff.

"How do you propose we do this?" Gabriel wanted to exhaust her logic so she'd give up on this nonsense.

"We sell their existing crap so they can buy the new stuff they want." She gave a flick of her hair to emphasise the sentence.

"Hmmm. I like that. Nice twist. But who's going to buy their old crap?" Gabriel became interested. This was a new angle for him.

"People in the biggest shitholes on the planet. We start by getting petty dictator's and freedom fighter's weapons from India. Once we prove that our new customers will pay, we can source some of the better weapons from Russia or China or North Korea."

"Imbal, I love you and your brain but this is insane. North Korea? Russia? How do we do that?"

"Not as difficult as you think. Provided we have buyers, they will give us a chance. One chance, mind you. They need us as much or more than we need them. They'll sell us their crap, which will be better than the crap from India and a godsend to our new clients."

"Do we only sell crap?"

"No. We work our way up the ladder. It takes time and contacts, but after a few deals we'll get onto the radar of the people who matter. They'll come to us."

"How do you know so much?"

"Israeli intelligence. We know where the weapons come from and usually how they get from A to B. We only do something when it affects Israel."

"But aren't we helping terrorists by selling them guns?"

"By that logic, everyone's a terrorist," Imbal said. "The founders of Israel and America were deemed terrorists by the British. As were Ghandi and Mandela. It's not our fight. As long as they leave us alone, I don't see any problem selling these weapons."

"Imbal, you're amazing. If you didn't make me feel the way you do, I'd tell you you're crazy."

"Let me put it another way," she said while moving closer to him. "The perks of the business are twofold." She put her hand on the inside of his thigh and kissed him on the neck. "One, we earn enough money to get married and have children." She ran her hands the length of his leg and kissed him lightly on the lips. "And two, we have a lot of spare time between deals to make those children."

She swung her legs over and faced him. His hands were on her thighs, moving upwards slowly. She started unbuttoning his shirt and he hers. There was no more discussion required. They were getting into the arms business.

∞

The arms industry is peculiar. Each major producing nation such as the U.S., Russia, and China, and the secondary players such as Germany, Britain, and France, make weapons for their own consumption. They keep the best and most secret weapons for themselves to provide an offensive or defensive edge in the global and regional balance of power. All other weapons are sold to allies and acceptable third parties. Legislation is in place to ensure countries don't inadvertently sell to their enemies. But the issue is relatively moot. Every purchaser on the planet can find a willing seller. In some ways, it is similar to pyramid marketing with the primary producing nations on the top and the entire global populace at the base. As with all pyramids, the base supports the whole.

"Can you believe Adoleke? What nerve. We gave him everything he wanted. I think he wants to go into business for himself," Gabriel said.

"I agree. He's dangerous. I'll have a word with our friends in the company. They may be interested to know that our new friend is channelling weapons to Egypt with a final destination of Gaza." Imbal never said Mossad, the Israeli secret service; she always referred to them as the company. Once identified, Adoleke would likely just disappear or find himself the victim of an unfortunate accident.

"How do the Arabs get all of those weapons? They must be getting help from higher up," Gabriel said.

"Yeah. It's disturbing to me too. The more we learn about this business, the less we know. We know someone is pulling the strings behind the scenes. What we don't know is who or how."

"That's a scary thought. But if so, we should be able to find out and neutralise them."

"We do know, more or less. But we can't neutralise. They're almost untouchable."

"Who are they? Gangsters? Mafia? No one is untouchable."

"The Americans, the Russians, the Chinese, the North Koreans, the Iranians. We're too small of a nation to dance with those powers. We have to pretend these actions are random but they're not. It's not an accident when our enemies are given such weapons."

"But we're making ourselves safer in what we're doing. The enemies of Israel can fight amongst themselves, as long as they don't turn on us." Gabriel always saw the dangers. This wasn't a natural business for him to be in. It didn't match his personality. He loved peace and dreamed of a world without wars.

"Wouldn't it be great if we could be part of the iron dome or something at that level? Think of the contacts." Imbal's eyes glowed.

"I think that's out of our league, don't you?"

"Why? We could market the system to countries around the world who want to stop incoming rockets and missiles. It would be a major step in peace. Missiles would become obsolete."

"Until they figure a way to trick the technology."

"Who cares?" said Imbal. "They'll always come up with more dangerous weapons. Let's see if we can be part of this."

"Ever since that summer, you wanted to be part of the dome."

"Ever since that summer, I realised I couldn't sit back and let this happen to us. We need to be players on this stage." Imbal believed this. It was the only way to face the anger and sense of helplessness she felt.

"Who do we call?"

Imbal smiled. They were young. They used that as an asset because few suspected them. They had just learned they were going to have a son. Their first born. They couldn't be happier.

Chapter Four

THE BOMBER
Moscow, Russia,
2 February, 2024

"Can I see your passport and boarding pass please?" The voice was formal but relaxed. She had been on this job for just over a year and all excitement around meeting famous people and good looking guys had faded. It was a bus station in the sky and she was the ticket monitor. *Besides, what I do is of no consequence,* she thought. The security guys would scan the travellers, their bags, and anything else that could be checked.

Tim Bull handed his passport and boarding pass to the woman, looked into the camera, and waited for the facial recognition to allow him past. Airports had a lot of security and part of this was creating unique identifications for each passenger and then cross referencing them with pretty much everyone to see if patterns emerged. If a red flag was thrown, he would be pulled aside and given a more intense review.

"Thank you, sir, and have a nice flight." The ticket and passport were handed back and she forgot Tim and was looking at the next person in the queue.

There were a number of people being processed at security. Twelve teams of security analysists were examining the contents of bags, jackets, and shoes on a conveyer belt through the X-ray machines. A seriously bored guy sat slumped in front of his screen, flipping between high and low frequencies and monitoring organic materials or anything that could be combined to create an explosive device.

"You want my shoes as well?" Tim said in English.

"Yes sir. Any laptop? That'll need to be taken out separately and put here." A tray was produced and Tim's laptop was placed inside. He had a jacket, belt, and the laptop bag. All went into plastic containers and through the X-ray machine.

"Come through." The security officer in a white shirt motioned at him. He was wearing tight black gloves. There was a woman next to him, presumably to pat down female passengers.

Tim stepped through the familiar rectangular personal scanner. There was no beep. He had done this many times before. He looked at the security guy and motioned with his palms up and a slight shrug to see if it was okay to proceed.

"Step over here please," the security officer said. "Do you mind using the full body scanner?"

"Of course not," Tim said. "I prefer it. As far as I'm concerned, the more security the better."

"Stand with your feet that way." He pointed to two blue footprints on the bottom of the round floor. "Put your arms up. Good, now stand still." Tim did and the doors closed on the glass cylinder and two sweeping scanning arms scanned his body. He would appear naked to someone in another room. They would be able to see anything he carried on him.

The door opened and Tim walked out. The security guy nodded and indicated with his hand towards Tim's computer and jacket on the conveyer belt. Tim gathered them, put on his shoes and belt, and made his way inside to wait for his flight.

As he sat with a coffee, he reflected on what had just happened. He did it. He knew what he needed to do next. As he sipped his coffee, he looked at the departures monitor. Stockholm boarded in thirteen minutes.

∞

Stockholm, Sweden,
7 February, 2024

Fredrick Johansen was retired, widowed, and ready to die. His life had no meaning and he had achieved what he hoped to during his eighty-three years. He knew many people like himself. Thousands. Alone, un-wanted, useless members of society. *All people want is for us to die*, Fred thought.

When he met Tim, Fred was looking into the morality and logistics of self-euthanasia. Suicide was no longer illegal but he had no intention of being found at the end of a rope or being shovelled up off a sidewalk. He wanted his death to mean something. As in life, he wanted to impact the world around him. After talking to Tim and getting to know him, Fred believed he had found a solution.

"You want to do what?" Fred asked. It was disbelief with a bit of a smile. His dentures showed slightly.

"I want to do something that will educate the world once and for all that their systems of oppression and war will not lead to peace. It is a statement that will not and cannot be ignored. Something so big they will be talking about it a century from now. Maybe even a millennia from now."

"Sounds intriguing but what can a couple of old farts like us achieve? What could we do to create such a mark?"

"You have heard about the self-immolation of the Buddhists, where they would douse themselves in fuel and set themselves alight. My idea is something like that but at a much grander scale. The morality of it may be questionable but the impact will be like nothing the world has ever seen." Tim's eyes shone. He was only seventy-four but arthritic and in constant pain. His hands were gnarled and full of blue veins pushing against improbably thin skin. Brown liver spots were on his temples and hands and most other places on his body. But when he talked about this, he felt no pain.

"What do you have in mind?"

"We need to be careful. We need to be paranoid. We need to treat this like the Americans treated their research on the atomic bomb in the desert during World War II. Ideally, I need another thousand or more people like us who we could get together and who no one would miss if they were to simply disappear for a year. Do you think that would be possible?"

"I think so. I assume they can't have any family? No living relatives?"

"Ideally not. Our candidates should not have a spouse or children and should be near death's door. I don't mind if they are incontinent or on crutches, wheelchairs, or stretchers. Our main criteria is trustworthiness and being decrepit." Tim said this and smiled. Fred smiled involuntarily.

"This sounds crazy," Fred said. "I love it. Where do I sign?"

"Hold on," Tim said. He was serious. "I need to tell you something before I tell you the plan. I need help to do this, so I trust you. But you are not to tell a soul. None of our recruits, no one. Otherwise, they'll not be able to do it when the time comes."

"Understood. Sounds ominous," Fred said.

"It is. Very serious stuff. We'll take our recruits to a retreat where they'll receive an operation and then recover for up to six months. It'll be warm, sunny, and we'll have pretty girls and boys to take care of them. Massages, great food, even sex if that's what they desire. But they'll be needed for a mission after that. We'll tell them they're to meet with various dignitaries around the world. They'll need to be able to fly. We'll ensure that they fly first class with all of the comforts. When they arrive, we'll give them their instructions."

"Doesn't sound too difficult," Fred said. "What are the operations for?" He didn't seem to be phased by finding innocent recruits and giving them unknown operations.

"I'll tell you shortly. The most important thing is that we find the right people and that they have a year to give us. We'll treat them well. As far as they are concerned, they will be part of a global lobby for the elderly. A G8 of sorts, but instead of a group of nations, this will be a group of geriatrics. We'll educate them on the way in which we, as a group, are discarded globally after giving our lives to societies. We fight their wars, build their companies, and provide them with our replacements through reproduction, and then we're discarded as obsolete and unwanted after we outlive our usefulness."

Fred found himself nodding. "True enough. I think you'll be preaching to the choir."

"I'm certain of it. Our primary weapon within democracies is the vote. We vote and we're heard. But we want the world leaders to do more. We need to create a global voice. This group would be that voice."

Fred was still nodding. "That's all fine and I'm sure you'll create the necessary glossy pages to keep them fooled. But what's the real reason?"

Tim liked this. He had done a lot of research before he found Fred. Ex-Swedish Special Forces, Fred was the picture of a model citizen. Below the surface, he was cynical, miserable, and distrustful. Most importantly, he was suicidal. This made him perfect. Tim adjusted his seat and told Fred his real plan.

When Tim finished, Fred had a faraway look in his eyes. "Are you sure we could pull something like this off?"

"There are some logistical issues to getting people around the world and synchronising everything. I am hoping to hit up to a thousand planes. Even if we hit half that number, we're talking about over a hundred thousand people dead, not to mention the economic impact. I'm just not sure how we're going to get a thousand people scattered around the world and in the air all at once." Tim sat back, pleased at Fred's reaction.

"We can figure it out," Fred said. "We target the largest hubs and divide the people accordingly. Long haul flights will only fly from the hubs. Frankfurt, London, Atlanta, Beijing are no brainers, but Moscow,

Paris, Madrid, Mexico, Buenos Aires, hell, any of the global cities will have long haul flights."

"Okay," said Tim, "but how do we get everyone to go along without knowing what they're doing?"

"I have an idea," said Fred. "Let's let that one sit. How about money?"

"I've worked my entire life," Tim said. "I've saved a small fortune by most people's standards. I have no one to give it to, nothing I believe in, and I wouldn't want to see those cocksuckers at the tax office get it as a gift. We should have enough to house, feed, and take care of a couple of thousand potential candidates. We do the procedure at the retreat and they can heal for at least six months before the appointed day." What Tim didn't tell Fred about was his silent partner and co-financier, the person who dreamed up this plan with him. His name was Jack and he was the biological son of Tim's oldest and most trusted friend, Joe. They had been in the CIA together and served in the jungles of 'Nam. They helped each other from time to time and he owed his life to Joe. When Jack contacted him, Tim didn't hesitate.

"Where's the retreat?"

"Spain. I picked up an entire abandoned village. It has been seventeen years since the market collapsed and it was simply there for the taking. My financial advisor just about had a stroke when I told him what I needed my money for. No, I didn't tell him the plan, just the purchase of the property. I told him I was thinking of opening a senior retirement community complete with medical facilities. I told him I'd make a fortune out of it."

"Wait," Fred said. "That's brilliant. We don't need to recruit. Your facility will attract everyone we need."

"Yes, but they'll have families and so on. We still need to find those with no connections."

"Understood. I'll figure something out. Up here in Sweden it's not too tough to find people who want to try living in the sun, especially if we run a promotional deal to lure them in."

"And we can screen the candidates. If anyone asks, it's a private facility and we can promote it to whomever we want. We specialise in providing a family to those who have no one else."

"And the procedure? How do you know it'll work?"

"Because I've already done it. I've been travelling with it in me for the last three months. Just came from Moscow and not even a blip—even with the body scanners."

Fred was alarmed. "You… you have it *in* you? Already?"

"Yes, but no timer. Just the product. Just to see if it would clear security. No problem on any front. I initially thought of having it in a colostomy bag but I was concerned the explosive sweeps would catch it. The safest place is inside the body."

"Because who suspects a geriatric bomber?" laughed Fred.

Tim and Fred worked through the logistics and bounced ideas off each other, but the heavy lifting had already been done by Tim. The facility was in place, the explosive material was purchased, and the procedure of putting it inside each bomber was tested and was successful. There was only one uncertain element: the mechanism by which the membrane separating the two liquid materials would break, causing the violent explosion. Tim had foreseen this and had commissioned an established Swiss clock maker to create a prototype for his new invention. He convinced the Swiss firm that he was looking to manufacture and sell medical clocks to go inside the body. All he needed was a working prototype. The firm was doubtful about the longevity of any such clock made solely of plastic but confirmed that it could be made. Tim's primary concern was the ability to puncture the membrane at a synchronised time.

"So you really want to do this?" Fred said after all the logistics had been worked through. "You realise we've already broken a whole lot of laws just talking the way we have, not to mention your actions. I'm now complicit. We would both go to jail just with what we've done so far. But we can stop and end this now if you want. No one needs to know."

"You're not having second thoughts?"

"No. Not at all. I'm getting a kick out of this. It makes me feel alive."

"I'm not a terrorist," Tim said. "I'm trying to shake awake the people of the world. They're like a bunch of zombies, following a path simply because no alternative has been presented. Yes, many will die, but the world doesn't notice unless it's shocking. But the greatest shock will be the lack of any political message. No country is attacking another. No religion is attacking another. Just a group of old people at the end of their lives sending a message to start living."

"Better a random, senseless killing than war," Fred said.

"Exactly. Cheaper, too, in terms of lives. Fewer lives lost and no one to blame. It'll be like putting a mirror up to all of the war mongers and makers of weapons."

"What if they don't see?" Fred said.

"Then they don't see. Screw 'em." Tim said. "You can lead a horse to water but you can't make it drink. The type of citizens the world needs are those who, when confronted with the end of the barrel of a gun, says 'screw you' to the person. I want the world to know that I just want to be left alone to live my life and pursue my own happiness. I don't want to hurt anyone. But if the world wants to take away my freedoms one by one, thinking I'll be like a frog in water, they have another thing coming. I do this because the next generation will not be able to. The world is breeding cowards and academics and bureaucrats, not thinkers or creators or doers. Even the thinkers are restricted to their corporate walls, and those are so few that they are nonexistent.

"I don't want any more war on this planet. I want people to see that a cornered rat can do as much damage as a nuclear bomb." Tim was getting worked up as he got into this. "We all agree that we need rules and government and military and a justice system and money and banking, but we don't need war fed to the weak to feed the strong."

"Ah, Tim," Fred said tentatively. "Aren't we buying the weapons of war from those same people you hate so much? Otherwise how could we buy the product going inside the people?"

Tim paused. "You're right, but I didn't buy from those manufacturing weapons. It's a chemistry problem and I have enough training to know that as long as the two substances don't meet, there won't be an explosion. Life is all about risk. I'll take this risk. I'll procure this myself."

"Those who manufacture weapons are government sanctioned firms, aren't they?" Fred asked.

"Amen. Have you noticed how many Toyotas just happen to end up in the hands of bad guys? Along with rocket launchers, machine guns, and a host of weapons. As the conflict increases in intensity, the purveyors of arms increase the power of weapons sold. Throughout the world, you see starving people carrying weapons they couldn't afford on a year's salary. They take, kill, and destroy. Countries need to make arms to protect themselves. Yes, I agree 100%, but it should be deemed an act of war for one country to sell weapons to another—even among allies—because the proliferation of weapons creates war. Otherwise, we would just be screaming at each other. We would have handfuls of dead instead of tens of thousands with rubble where there used to be infrastructure." Tim pushed aside the beer and poured himself some whiskey.

"Careful with that whiskey. It's homemade hooch from a guy I know."

"Will I go blind?"

"Not from that," Fred laughed. "At least not immediately."

The topic changed from war and death to a much more enlightened discussion of how they were going to wake up the world—with a whole lot of death. Neither of them saw it as ironic. Time would tell if they were right.

∞

"Security systems do not rely solely on scans by machines," Tim said. They were contemplating how much to tell their geriatric bombers. "A security officer should look at the behaviour of the potential passenger. It's why good security in airports require passengers to wait as long as possible to be processed. It gives the officers time to analyse the people. Sweating, nervousness, mumbling prayers, even being freshly shaved can be triggers. Being too clean, too happy, too perfect can also be a trigger."

Fred liked this. "The slob with earrings, long hair, and headphones may be less of a threat than a sharply dressed businessman in a $5,000 suit?"

"Exactly. Depending on the circumstances. Combined with a personal interview by at least one but usually two officers, a passenger must pass the gut test. Are they trying too hard to be normal?"

"So," said Fred, "this is why we must ensure our people are oblivious to their true purpose. As far as these poor fish are concerned, they're part of some global lobbying force. A global initiative, if you will, which requires them to co-ordinate their presence on flights around the world. We'll need to come up with a good reason."

"What good reason do people need?" Tim said. "We're going to take care of them in a luxury resort, do whatever surgery they need (with a little of our own special sauce), and make them feel like humans again. We suggest for them to participate in our programme and they get to fly to exotic places in the world first class. What do they have to complain about? Those who don't agree can stay home. We just need to prepare a sufficient number so that our volunteers will meet our requirements."

Tim's talking as though these people are cattle while telling himself he's fighting for their rights to be treated like humans, Fred thought. "And what are we demanding of the world?" he asked.

"We should demand transparency of ownership and involvement of anyone dealing with arms manufacturing and sales. This should be made public and available to any citizen. There should be no sales of weapons above police grade to foreign countries. Countries should make their own weapons or invite the manufacturers into their country to protect them—using their own blood instead of locals. The last thing we need is another form of militant colonialism let in through the back door. Weapons must cease to be the only unregulated currency. It is the currency of war and global destabilisation. No foreigner is to use a weapon unless made by their own country. Breach should be a war crime."

Chapter Five

THE PASSENGER
London, England,
25 June, 2025

The sound of the road made a rhythm in Josie's head. The four lanes of the M25 stretched before her, separated by the headrests of the front seat and, of course, the glass of the taxi's windshield. It was a mini cab and not specifically a taxi. They weren't allowed to stop and pick up casual passengers, only reservations. Some of the mini cabs were quite old and had smells of family and other lives because the driver used the family car for the job. But this cab was spotless. It was a Peugeot something or other and, for Josie, felt like a mid-ranged Mercedes in the back. She was heading to Heathrow and they needed to use the M25, a 120 mile perimeter highway that circled greater London. When it worked, cars flew along at 80 miles per hour. Few in the fast lane bothered with the 70 mile speed limit. Besides, every system allowed for at least a 10% tolerance. To combat this, governments put in place an average speed limit that meant cameras taking pictures of you at one point and then again at another point miles away and calculating your speed. There was no way to slow down for the camera and speed up afterwards. You had to follow the speed limit. The best way to know if the cameras were working was to follow the traffic. If everyone (including the fast lane) was driving 70, then the cameras were working and you needed to comply.

"Going anywhere nice today?" the cab driver asked.

"Going home for the summer holidays," Josie said.

"And where's home?" the cab driver said, trying to generate a conversation.

"Buenos Aires, Argentina. Unfortunately, it's cold there now."

"Sounds lovely."

"Have you just started your shift?" Josie wanted to change the subject. She already disliked his robotic replies. Who says 'sounds lovely' after you just described your destination as being 'cold'? She really didn't want to talk.

"Started 5am this morning. I'll have a couple more rides after yours and then I'm off."

"Sounds like hard work. How long before we get to Heathrow?"

"Depending on traffic, another forty minutes or so."

"Okay, thanks." She looked at her phone and went through her emails, texted a few friends, and updated her social media. Everyone already knew she was going to Argentina but she felt obliged to keep her status up to date wherever people may look. *I just wish Pepe was coming with me*, she thought. She put that thought out of her mind. It wasn't happening and she needed to move on with her life.

She closed her eyes and waited for Heathrow to arrive. At that point, the car slowed down for the QEII Bridge across the Thames. The radio referred to it as the Dartford crossing and it was historically a pinch point for traffic. Two tunnels went under the Thames counter clockwise and the bridge went over the Thames clockwise.

"You know," said the cabbie, "this was supposed to be free as of 2003 because the tolls paid for the bridge construction. Then the government changed its mind and continued the toll. Eventually they raised the rates. They are now taking in over £115 million a year from it."

"Uh huh," mumbled Josie. She couldn't care less. She also didn't like heights so she preferred to have her eyes closed as they crossed the suspension bridge.

∞

It seemed dream-like to Josie from that point until she was sitting in her seat on the British Airways 777 nonstop direct flight. She had splurged and upgraded to business class. The trip was almost fourteen hours of flying and she wanted to be able to sleep. She worked hard and her annual trip home was something she wanted to enjoy. She looked forward to her mother's cooking and her father's moustachioed kisses. Her parents were getting old now and video calls over the internet only took you so far. She wanted their smells and their hugs as well as their conversation.

"Excuse me, dear." An elderly woman nudged Josie. "Can I get past? Sorry to be a bother."

Josie looked up and saw a blue-wash-haired lady who must have been almost eighty. She was ambulatory but her movements were cautious and she had a genuine smile on her face. "Of course. One moment." Josie got up and stood aside as the old woman shuffled past. She smelled of baby powder and a slightly sharp old fashioned perfume. She wore Nike trainers and something like a high end set of sweat pants and jacket. *So much for getting dressed up for flying*, thought Josie.

The woman saw Josie looking at her clothes and said, "It's a long flight and I need to be comfortable at my age. I'm long past the stage where I worry about how I look." She smiled and Josie smiled back.

"No, not at all," said Josie. "I was just thinking of what a good idea it was," she lied. She didn't want to be sitting awkwardly next to this person for the whole trip.

In fact, Josie would not be sitting next to this person at all. It would only be four hours and thirty-five minutes into their flight when she wasn't sitting next to anyone, or even sitting. Her, her neighbour, and everyone else on the plane ceased to exist as the membrane between her neighbour's internal payload was breached. The Swiss plastic clock worked as planned and Tim's homemade chemistry experiment went off. The plane, crew, and 361 passengers perished above a disinterested ocean, along with 762 other planes worldwide at that precise moment.

Chapter Six

MARK AND LEANNE
United States,
26 June, 2025

Sable nuzzled Mark as the daylight entered his ground floor apartment. He had some outside space allocated specifically to him. His patio outside his sliding doors was made of treated green wood large enough for a BBQ, round table with four chairs, and some socialising space for when he would have some guests over. As part of his insurance settlement, his advisors urged him to buy an apartment with some outside space and try to live on one level. Mark replied that he wasn't a cripple, just a survivor of a head on collision. It was just unfortunate that one of the heads was his and the other was the grill of a muscle car. He bought a safe apartment in a safe neighbourhood with his own patio and green grass.

"That's my girl," Mark said to Sable. "How'd you sleep?"

Sable replied by nuzzling him more urgently.

"You need to go out?" He realised this just in time. He opened the door. "Out you go. Good girl."

Sable turned out to be just what Mark needed. They walked in the park next to the animal shelter and returned within the hour. He decided to name her after her colouring and the French name for sand. Mark agreed to take Sable home and she let him be her master.

Mark smiled when he looked at the young dog's energy. There was no hatred in her and her movements were so smooth, so powerful. It was as though she glided above the ground. They came home after picking up some dog essentials and he took the chance that she was house trained. *So far so good*, he thought.

"You know the main problem with you," Mark said to Sable upon her return into the apartment, "is that people will start thinking I'm crazy for talking to myself. But I'm talking to you. See, it's already happening." He reached down and gently ran his hand over her head and scratched deftly behind her ear. Sable wanted to jump up on him but he told her to stay down. She then came up to him, cat-like, and pushed her body against his leg. He laughed and kneeled down to give her a proper scratch and full back pat. Sable's back leg quivered when he touched certain parts of her ear and back.

Mark prepared her breakfast, a full bowl of dry dog-food that would always be topped up. He didn't want her to be hungry and start scavenging. She could always know that she has enough food. He gave her a tin of wet food too. He didn't want to know what went into it but he knew it was healthier than what a lot of humans ate. He also filled her water bowl. Sable waited patiently and then demolished the wet, nibbled the dry, and took a long drink from the water bowl. A smacking of her chops and she was ready for more attention from Mark.

The television was on from the moment he woke. Global air traffic was grounded until further notice. Militaries around the world were on high alert, all reservists were called in, and politicians of all shades wore sombre faces. There were the unending grim pictures of exploded planes on runways and pictures of relatives waiting for their loved ones who would never arrive; pictures of search and rescue missions with eyes looking out the windows in vain over the cold unforgiving oceans. Pictures of a global war without a clear enemy.

It was at 15:00 GMT when a one line message was received by the world's largest intelligence gatherer, the CIA. It had been delivered to the United Nations' headquarters in New York in the form of an email to each delegate. The CIA was furious it had not ferreted out the message first. It read simply: "This is not the end. Learn from this."

This set the world's newscasters into a frenzy. Where was it sent from? Germany, apparently, but no-one could confirm anything. Yes, joint forces representing all of the affected nations were working co-operatively to find out who did this. Yes, the IP address was being chased, and yes, the providers opened up full access to their networks to assist in this manhunt. No, it was not known when the state of emergency would be lifted. And no, there were no suspects.

What wasn't reported was the chemical residue found on the remains of the planes and victims on the ground, which the forensic teams determined to be the cause of the explosion. In a handful of cases, they were able to identify the source of the blast as the first class and business class part of the planes. Flight manifests were being analysed and cross referenced to see who would become a suspect. From there, the teams would find links to the world of the living and recreate the carnage. Explosions created a blast of such intensity that even the planes on the ground exploded, their fuel situated in the wings catching fire. In some cases, planes parked next to the explosions caught fire and created a macabre series of explosions, domino style, in front of waiting passengers.

Mark watched the television absent-mindedly while finishing his second cup of coffee. He ground the beans into a talcum-like dust before making an espresso in one of those aluminium pots that sat on the element to heat up. Luckily, he had gas and it heated quickly. He preferred this coffee partly because he liked the comfort of his own home and because he wanted to enjoy the simple pleasures of life. The events of yesterday reinforced his feeling of being alive. Good coffee and good food were important.

When he had enough of the chaos and depression on the television, he grabbed the leash. The sound of the leather and the clink of the chain's clip as it knocked against the wall where it was hung made Sable's head pop up and she came running. She didn't have a tail so her entire body wagged from the middle.

He clipped her to the leash and opened the door. It was beautiful outside, barely a cloud in the sky with a slight breeze. It was idyllic. Who would have thought that almost a quarter million people had lost their lives needlessly in the worst attack in history? Despite the loss of life and property—some reckoned it to be in excess of $2 trillion—many strategists had a begrudging respect to the mastermind behind it. Mark put the talking heads out of his own and enjoyed the pure joy of walking outside with Sable, where a mouldy leaf or another dog's urine could be the highlight of the day.

He made his way to the park, where he hoped she would behave sufficiently to let her off the leash. He knew she needed to run and burn off some energy, play with some other dogs, and enjoy her freedom. He also knew that he could stop by Luigi's on the way home to pick up some pizza.

"Fancy seeing you here," a familiar woman's voice said. He didn't see her immediately but turned and smiled.

"Hi Leanne. I'm glad we bumped into each other." He couldn't say anything else because she had stopped listening and was bent next to Sable. She was holding her head in her hands and talking to it like she was a baby—and Sable loved it. The dog tried licking Leanne, who gave little kisses to Sable's soft fur along the side of her snout and above the lips. Sable started wagging her body again.

"What a beautiful creature," she cooed. "What's her name?"

"Sable. Just got her yesterday."

Leanne shifted her weight onto one leg and curved her body as she looked at Mark. "Lovely name." She shook her head slightly and the rest of her body fol-lowed suit. He tried to not notice. *She is fit and everything moves as it should*, he said to himself.

"Where you off to?"

"The park then back to pick up some pizza at Luigi's."

"Sounds like fun. I'd love to join you sometime. Maybe I'll crash your pizza party and see you later."

"Seriously?" Mark regretted saying it as it came out. He wasn't sure if it sounded like he was making fun of her or goading her to firm up a date.

"Of course." She didn't take any notice of the word or tone. "Here, take my card. When you arrive at

Luigi's, give me a call and I'll pop over. We can go to wherever you were planning to eat the pizza—but I'll join you. I hope that's okay?"

"Better than okay," Mark said. "I'll give you a call then. See ya in a bit."

And that's how you do it, he said to himself. Sable wasn't the only one gliding above the ground.

∞

"So what exactly do you do that allows you to meet up with strange men and eat pizza with them in their home?" Mark still had some pizza in his mouth. Sable sat rigidly still, the saliva gathering and drooling from the edges of her lips. She would occasionally lick her lips in a sweeping motion but the saliva was definitely winning. She watched Mark's hand as it went from the box to his mouth and back to his plate. For his part, Mark was wondering how long he could restrain himself from feeding her. She was *really* good at begging.

"I work at the family business. My parents were the engines of the whole thing and were into trade. They took their profits and bought prime property. I'm just watching the paint dry and ensuring that the buildings are still there, that the rent is paid, and that all the properties are maintained by the tenants. We have some residential but mostly high end commercial and retail space. If you think about it, my job is just to not screw things up. I don't actually *do* anything." She took another bite of the pizza. Mark had purchased a spicy peperoni as well as a plain cheese pizza—just in case. She ate the peperoni.

"Sounds like a nice situation," Mark said. "I'm still wondering what I'm going to do. But first, I need to get strong again. No sense getting ahead of myself. That's why I got Sable." He rubbed the begging dog behind the ears. She initially thought a treat was coming her way and followed Mark's hand and then snapped back to staring at Leanne, bits of white saliva getting on Mark's sleeve. "Hopefully I'll be in a position to start settling into a normal life in the coming months. Everything seems so big, fast, and alive. Much more than I remember."

"Sounds fascinating. Like taking a decade long nap. Do you feel like a Rip Van Winkle?"

"You're not the first to ask me that. I feel exactly the same, but my body's weak. I can see that I've aged. I don't know any of the current music or news but even that doesn't seem to make much of a difference. The biggest change is my indifference to current events. I've heard people talk about being hyper connected, never being able to shut off their social media channels. It makes me feel like I shouldn't even join in. A bit like watching others doing cocaine, knowing it's better to just pass and look like a nerd."

"Funny. I've never had it explained like that before." Leanne looked at her phone. "It's like an extension of me. I'm not sure if I could function without it."

"Maybe you should try it for a bit."

"I don't think I could and still be responsible at the firm."

"I thought you said you were watching paint dry," Mark said.

"Well, I may have been exaggerating my lack of activity. My parents have introduced me into the trading element these last couple of years and I'm finding it fascinating. Now with what is going on in the world, that element represents the biggest engine for growth for us."

"What kind of trading?"

"Mainly manufactured goods from rich to poor countries. We tend to use ships so the plane transport crisis everyone's facing doesn't affect us."

"Sounds complicated," Mark said.

"Not really. Just contacts and being trustworthy. Your customers need to know that you say what you mean and do what you say. Everything else seems to follow from that." She took a slug of Coke to wash down the pizza. *She doesn't look like a pizza and Coke kind of girl*, Mark thought.

He took a slug of Coke as well. He wasn't sure what to do at this point. He didn't know why she even came to his apartment. *Should I tell her to leave?*

As if reading his mind, Leanne said, "I should probably go but I would love to join you and Sable for a walk when you go next time."

"Sounds like a good plan. It'd be nice to have someone to talk to who talks back," Mark said. "I love to talk to Sable but I think people are starting to look at me funny."

"It's only been a day, Mark," she said. "Give it time. Then people will know something's funny with you." She smiled.

"We'll walk back with you," Mark said. "Sable looks like she needs more than just our morning stroll. We'll go to the park and watch the swans and the old codgers feeding the pigeons."

"She's really taken to you," she said. "Look at her. She's putty in your hands."

"The real reason may be the pizza. It may be that she's not sure whether I'm on the menu or just delivering the pizza to her." He got up and Sable followed his every movement with laser-like intensity. When he reached for the leash, even the pizza faded.

"It's times like these when you want someone to hold you in their arms and tell you things are going to be okay." She looked at Mark. "But I don't have anyone."

Sable whimpered slightly and pulled at the leash. Mark locked her gaze, again not sure what he should do. He would love to hold her against him now in a grand movie-like gesture but he felt it was too soon. Instead, he said, "You always have me, for what it's worth." Sable looked back at the two of them, increasingly impatient.

It seemed to do the trick. Leanne moved closer and hugged him. After a short time she pulled away. "Sorry. I needed that."

"My pleasure," Mark said, trying to be nonchalant. His body's temperature spiked, heart racing, and he felt a tremble from the adrenaline. "Shall we walk? Sable's wondering why we're neglecting her."

"Of course," she smiled, the mood lightening. "Let's go."

She was silent for a few minutes and then slipped her arm through his. It was gentle and almost natural. Mark allowed his elbow to jut out slightly. *Intimate and classy*, he thought. *Glad I didn't make a move on her earlier.* They walked that way for almost fifteen minutes. When it came to the point when Leanne should have gone left, she shook her head and they turned right towards the park. Once there, they kept to the edge of the paved walkway as joggers and the occasional cyclist passed. They stopped next to the pond with its swans and geese. There was a bench overlooking the water and they sat down. Mark looped Sable's leash to the bench's arm and she sat and then lay down next to their feet. Her nose was almost at Mark's feet, sitting neatly on her paws.

∞

The news readers recounted the previous day's events as further images of the recent disaster played in the background. *"It's been nearly forty-eight hours and authorities around the globe are no closer to under-standing the motive or means by which these terrible atrocities have been committed. The total death toll now stands at 276,822. It's impossible to express the loss of talent and energy to the world. Some of the world's greatest scientists, thinkers, politicians, and businesspeople have been lost senselessly. It's not just the loss of life, which is terrible, but the loss of confi-dence in the rhythm of modern life. It would be trite to say that this will leave an indelible scar on humanity. The financial loss to airlines means bankruptcy to al-most all of them. Each nation has stepped up and vowed to stand behind their airlines. The military has said it would make its planes available to allow interim service to essential civilian travel. All but the largest insurance companies have gone bust, seeking shelter behind bankruptcy legislation. Governments have vowed to honour the claims where possible. Banks have suffered their largest two day loss in history and governments have declared a bank holiday for the re-mainder of this week while systems are put in place..."*

Sable yawned, her tongue curling upwards as the jaws opened wide. She adjusted herself on her mattress bed and went back to sleep. Mark was making his morning coffee and Leanne was still in bed. He didn't know how she liked her coffee and didn't want to disturb her. Her phone was on the kitchen table. Her jacket lay across the chair, over her purse. It vibrated and went silent.

Mark looked over and saw a missed message. He moved it closer to the chair holding her jacket and purse.

It vibrated again. Another message. He looked towards the bedroom door and briefly at Sable. He had taken a sip of his coffee and had settled into his usual chair next to the table.

Her phone vibrated again. He picked it up and glanced at it. He swiped his finger across the bottom, knowing it would have a password. It didn't. The message displayed and he couldn't stop himself from reading it.

Chapter Seven

THE REVOLUTIONARY
United Kingdom, 27 June, 2025

It's started, Jason said to himself. He was bolted to the television set in his lounge. He channel-surfed all the stations from Al Jazeera, BBC, Sky, CNN, China Daily, and even Russia News. He monitored articles on the internet via Google and friended as many people as possible on Facebook. He knew in his heart that this was the same movement as his. *There will be suffering*, he thought, *but it will be for a just and good end.*

The world had just been informed of the message received via the UN delegates. Lacking anything else, it loomed as the only message from the dead terrorists.

This is not the end. Learn from this.

It is the anticipation of the decision by one's over-lord that creates the greatest tension in the recipient.

The stress faced once the decision has been made is a relief in comparison. The reason is simple: anticipation lurches the person from freedom to prison, torture to ecstasy. The punishments and rewards are limited only to the mind's imagination. And now this new terror group has expanded the world's imagination.

They are following the same logic as me. Strike at the most powerful. Strike once, go quiet. Don't get caught. Jason watched the television, clicked through sites on the internet, all the while cradling his mobile phone, allowing him to monitor the social media he signed up to. It was exhausting requiring him to drink endless Cokes and coffees to keep going. His diet consisted of takeaway Chinese, fried chicken, and ready meals bought frozen from the store in town. He hunkered down in his home with seven acres and watched. And waited. No one would be looking for him. His acts would fade into nothing next to the bombings.

But my message got out. It got coverage. People know, he thought. They will see this and know that the time has come. The real terrorists are the oppressive government bureaucracies that have become disconnected to the real people.

His phone rang.

"Hello?" Jason said, watching as the BBC did a summary of events. Again.

"Hi, Jay? It's Mum."

"Hi Mum," Jason said, struggling to pull away from the screens.

"I'm putting in a roast. All the others will be here. Will you be able to come?

"What's the occasion?" Jason said, a little perturbed. He enjoyed his cocoon of junk food and news.

"Does there need to be a reason? I'm your mother and I would like my family next to me. I don't want to see or hear about the terrible things in the world. I'm tired of only hearing about killing and the evil that men do. I want my loved ones next to me so I can feed them and tell them I love them."

There's no avoiding this, Jason thought. "Okay, Mum. When do you want me there?"

"As soon as," she said.

"Okay. Let me jump in the shower and I'll be right over."

"You're a good boy Jay," she said. "I love you."

"Love you too." He exhaled deeply. So much for wallowing. History would have to wait. Mum wants a sit down meal with her family.

"And how is the world going to cope with this new crisis? Surely this is nothing short of catastrophic for the airline industry and tourism in general." The voice of the interviewer filled the car as Jason made his way to his family's home. At least he'd be able to get in a good fix of news from BBC Radio 4 during his drive. Another voice said, *"Ironically, the super-rich were unaffected, as they tend to travel in private jets. The unintended consequences of these bombings was the widening of the gap between the rich and poor. Now,*

only the rich or very important will be able to fly. Gone are the days of planes being busses in the sky, available to every working person."

Amazing, thought Jason. *Who would've thought it?*

A woman's voice entered the discussion. *"We now know that 763 commercial planes were lost on Wednesday. It's a day that will go down in history. At an average cost of $350 million per plane, this one act of terrorism has eliminated over $260 billion dollars of aviation stock. It only takes three months to build a new plane, but if only one factory was building, it would take us 190 years to rebuild this fleet. Luckily, the world has more than one factory."* Nervous laughter amongst the guests. *"Even with overtime and government intervention, it will be years before we are anywhere near what we once were."*

The moderator interrupted. *"Do you think retired planes could be useful? Is that an option? Obviously, they would need some serious servicing, but is it even viable?"*

A heavily accented French voice joined in. *"The average age of a retired plane is twenty-five years. Some of the more affluent airlines may retire their planes earlier than that on policy grounds or because they want the newest technology. After twenty-five years, these planes have gone through a lot. That being said, there are still quite a number of commercial airplanes in service after forty years. It is possible but the issue is not technical; it is about the public trust. Will you feel safe putting your son or daughter on a plane—especially an old plane built during the Carter and Reagan administrations before the new generation of technology was adopted? I know I would think twice. Maybe take the car or cancel the trip or change business models."*

"That is exactly the type of talk that is propping up everywhere," the moderator said. *"The blow was not the loss of materiel; it was the loss of confidence in the technology and the security and the politicians in charge. Many are calling for a rethink of the entire..."*

The voice died when Jason turned off his car. His mother's home was a detached property set on two acres of land in an affluent suburb of London. Although no Londoner would consider her home a suburb, it was in the boon docks as far as those who inhabited the central zones were concerned. She was in the countryside, inside Greater London but almost as far cut as Surrey, in retirement and commuter land. If her home was in central London, it would have been worth £40 million or more; where it was, it was only worth £7 million. Downright penury for the city boys.

She was rather old fashioned but it was probably her sense of morality that was the origin of Jason's outrage against the government. He didn't share his frustrations with his mother or family. As far as they were concerned, he was living the life of Riley in exotic locations. They couldn't know the stresses and torments he suffered.

As he walked up the pebbled drive, the sounds of birds were all around him and the smell of a barbeque wafted from the back garden. His mother was a keen ornithologist and loved putting out feed for the song birds. She was not so keen on the neighbour's cat, who was a constant threat to her feathered friends, nor the squirrels that ate the birds' food. Her house was Victorian and very proper, not too much above their station but satisfactory for a solid upper middle class family. It was five bedroomed with a large lounge for entertaining and a decent sized dining room for eating. Mostly they ate in the recently redecorated Clive Christianson kitchen. It was a major upgrade and boasted the requisite granite countertops and splashbacks as well as all new appliances, covered by the burr oak finishes to match the rest of the design. Even the Aga was upgraded to allow for the four ovens and gas hob. She loved it.

Jason's father was manning the barbeque. It was a tradition during summer that they would eat burned meat. He refused to serve it unless he was certain everything was dead. There was no reasoning with him so each child learned to eat and smile. There were salads to help ease digestion but the most important condiment was the wine. *Good Bordeaux plonk*, his father would say, *makes even the worst food palatable.*

"I thought you were putting on a roast?" Jason said as he kissed his mother's cheek. He saw her through the kitchen window that overlooked the drive. There was no escaping the greeting ritual. He didn't mind.

"Don't be cheeky. Things changed." His mother replied. She was a little flushed but that may have been the wine. "I'm glad you came, Jay. The others are out back."

Jason went towards the garden and grabbed a beer. He'd have some wine later.

"Jason," his father's voice called from the grill. "Come here. I'd like to introduce you to someone."

He froze as he got up and saw who his father had next to him. It was Sir Harry Constable, the sonofabitch former secretary of state who started this whole nightmare for Jason.

"Hello, Sir," Jason said. He shook the proffered hand.

"Good to meet you, Jason. Please call me Harry. Your father has been telling me a lot about you."

"Hopefully only the good bits," Jason said, a little nervously.

"I lied like any proud parent," his father said. He was enjoying himself and must have already had a couple of beers as he prepared to cremate the steaks and sausages.

"I'm sure he didn't," said Harry. "Now tell me, Jason, what do you make of all this craziness lately? I'm a bit blinkered by the bubble in which I live."

"Oh," said Jason, "what is it you do?"

"I used to be heavily involved with politics, but now I'm a consultant helping people gain access to the government. It's a different approach to life and the perspective is not what I anticipated it to be."

"Sir Harry's being modest," said James' father. "You *must* remember him, Jay. He was the secretary of state, for goodness sake. It must've been around the same time that you were doing all of your business deals."

"Yes, I think I remember now. Sorry for not recognising you, Sir Harry. It must be a real insult for you." Jason's mind was racing. *How is this possible? Am I living some parallel existence?*

"Not at all," Harry chuckled. "It's a common misunderstanding. To tell you the truth, people think I was intimately involved in everything. It is the *office* of the secretary of state that knows all and sees all. I was just the figurehead to be admonished or praised, as is the will of the people. Naturally, I managed things, but 98% of everything in the office is done by the administrative staff. The infamous civil servants. You must be familiar with *Yes, Minister*?"

"Uh, yes. A bit before my time. I understand Margaret Thatcher was a keen watcher and enjoyed it immensely." Jason was disoriented. *Was it possible this man who he vilified and launched a revolution against was wholly ignorant of his very existence?*

"Yes, yes. Apparently it was something that really got to her. Hit her funny bone, they say." Harry was seemingly oblivious of Jason.

"Dad, how do you and Sir Harry know each other?" He couldn't control his curiosity.

"Old school chums. Eton, then Oxford. Best years of my life," his father said.

"And why haven't I seen or heard about this before?" Jason couldn't help but ask.

"Because that's what mates do. They allow their friends to get on with things. We managed to meet up at the club and a few functions here and there. Nothing more than a few days a year. But I really am honoured with your presence here today, Sir Harry. Thank-you." *He must have had more than just a couple drinks*, Jason thought.

"Not at all, Jim. It really has been too long since I've spent time with you at your home. Maybe that's part of why I'm here. These last few days have been so hectic. What with the crazy assassin—some people think he really wanted to kill me—and the global bombings, life seems so fragile, so impermanent. I was heading out of town anyway and thought I'd swing by and visit ol' Jim."

Jason's father was touched and he cleared his throat. "Thanks Harry. It means a lot to me for you to say that." Jason noticed the lack of 'Sir' in his father's last remarks. Perhaps they really were friends.

Jason made an excuse to see his brothers and drifted away from the two older men. He was in shock. He had killed three people, announced a revolution, and carried a cancerous hatred in his gut for a man and a system that was wholly indifferent to him. Was he so narcissistic as to be unaware of reality? Could he have been so wrong?

Chapter Eight

Leanne's Story

Leanne Darcy Holmes was born on September 11, 1993, into an upper middle class white American family. Her mother was educated at one of the top prep schools in Milton, Massachusetts, while her father was educated not too far away in Andover's Phillips Academy. Leanne was a legacy student in Milton Academy and made the most of the contacts it brought her. It was a world where the future was incubated and encouraged to flourish in class sizes of fewer than eight. It was an idyllic upbringing where one's future was truly as great as one's imagination.

It was on her eighth birthday when those planes flew into those buildings all those years ago. She was protected from the worst of the rhetoric but she was precocious and found her life changed by the event. Her parents became more serious and more political. A tipping point was reached when the first invitation to the White House was received.

"Did you see the stationary?" Lea said. She and her mother shared the same name. For ease, only Leanne was called by her full name. "And the envelope? Lovely. Feel it Hank."

"Lovely, sweetheart. But I think we'll be talking about more serious matters."

"I know, but let me enjoy this. Can you believe it, Leanne? You mother and father will be meeting the president of the United States in the White House!" She was acting like she had just won the Miss Universe beauty competition. She beamed as she made her way from the kitchen to the lounge and then upstairs to check on something in their bedroom, only to repeat the process again.

"Relax," Hank said. "They're only meeting us because they need us."

"Even better," she said. "Who would've thought? Lea and Hank Cummings, guests of the president?"

"It's a business transaction. We're there to assist in making America safer. We'll play our role, that's it."

"Oh, don't be such a stick in the mud," said Lea. "Whatever we are, we've got the backing of the president of the United States of America."

By the time she turned eighteen, the novelty had worn off. In fact, she started seeing less and less of her parents. They were constantly on international business trips to London or Geneva. She found it odd when they came back tanned in the middle of winter from London—and not just tanned, burned.

Leanne was good at mathematics and found herself in a joint JD/MBA programme at Harvard. It was partly due to her inability to choose between law and commerce. This degree gave her the best of both worlds, and it was Harvard.

"Now that you've got your degree, I think it's about time that you think about working. Have you given this any thought?" Lea enjoyed their Sunday morning teas. The sun came through the conservatory windows and made the white linen table cloth glow.

"I would like to see a bit of the world before I settle down," Leanne said. "I know you and Dad are waiting for me to take over your empire but I'm still too young."

"I agree whole heartedly," said Lea. "What would you like to do?"

"I'm not entirely sure and I don't want my education to go to waste. It would be nice to see Europe and China and Russia."

"And South America and Africa?" added Lea.

"I don't know how much time I have," said Leanne smiling. "Are you funding this or am I?"

"Do we ever say 'no' to you, sweetheart?" Her father came in and sat down. "I would like you to travel with someone, definitely not alone. And I would like to have a schedule of where you are at all times so we can be in touch."

"Yes sir," Leanne said. "And would you like to chip and pin me at the same time?"

"Who says we haven't already?" Hank said, smiling.

"I agree with your father. Safety has to be a consideration. I am all for expanding your horizons and the world is a big place. Now is the right time to travel, but we want you to be safe."

"I'll talk with some of my friends. Maybe a couple will want to join me. Round the world tickets and a year travelling shouldn't be too hard to sell." Leanne was already picturing herself in Rome with an espresso, newspaper, and a steamy hot Italian lover. She shook her head, laughing at her own nonsense.

"That sounds sensible, and you'll never get another chance like this later in life," her mother added.

"Just as long as you are safe and act responsibly," added her father.

"Sounds like a plan," said Leanne. "Oh, one last thing. Do I get to bring my black American Express card along?"

Her parents laughed. "We wouldn't want you to leave home without it."

When she returned, she was ready to begin her adult life. Travelling was okay up to a point, but eventually each place begins to look like the next. Each person you meet is a version of the last one. Each story you hear is an extrapolation of a handful of stories repeated in every corner of every city throughout the world.

Travel for the sake of travel had lost its appeal. She was ready for something more. Something that gave her actions meaning.

She returned to a family office, which oversaw a portfolio of assets but was focused on prime property in a handful of key cities. Total assets under management were pushing $400 million, but half of that was debt.

"We're not that big when you start looking at the sizes of other family offices," her father said. "We've created this office for you. Your mother's and my trading business has been kept separate. I don't want you worrying about the volatility that we face. Everything in this office will be yours and I would like you to start running it. Learn, act responsibly, and use this as a springboard to where you'd like to eventually find yourself."

"Dad, this is too much," Leanne said. "This is insane. I had no idea. Don't get me wrong, I'm in. All in. But, holy molly, this isn't what I was expecting last month sipping mate in Patagonia."

"You don't like it?"

"I love it. All. But I'm just taking it all in."

"We own the building we're in. It's not the best in the city but it's pretty good. It'll hold its value and provide you with the credibility to grow this into something spectacular."

"I love it, Dad. I love you."

Hank beamed. All of the work, risk, sacrifice, and toil was vindicated in this one moment. He just wished Lea could be with him. She'd just have to receive Leanne's praises over dinner that night.

∞

That was just over a dozen years ago and Leanne had put all of her energy into the family office. Her training was a perfect match and she was able to make some key acquisitions. She made some mistakes but nothing anyone outside the firm would have noticed. She was determined to make her parents proud. Along the way, she had her romantic interludes but nothing stuck. She felt that any suitor was treating her as a corporate merger instead of the love of their life.

She had everything else, and wanted love too, so when she felt Mark's touch gently shaking her awake, she found herself in new territory. Mark was a nobody when it came to money or power, but she found herself drawn to him. He was kind, sincere, and gentle. He didn't have any ulterior motives and made her feel beautiful. And he had a lovely dog.

"Hi."

"Hi." Mark was looking at her under the light cover, his hand gently placed on her hip. "I need to talk to you."

"I know. Last night was crazy…"

"No. Not that. Last night was perfect. You were perfect." Mark leaned over and kissed her on the lips. "I made some coffee. Do you want some?"

"It does smell great. Yes, please."

"Your phone has been vibrating non-stop for thirty minutes. Here." He didn't tell her that he read some of the messages.

"Thanks. I'll see you in the kitchen. I just need to wash my face."

"Okay. Take your time."

Mark returned to the kitchen. He braced himself for what was coming. It didn't take long.

"I have to go," Leanne said. She had gone white, her face gaunt and hair unbrushed.

"Is everything okay?" Mark asked.

"Yeah, everything's fine. I just received some news and I need to go home urgently."

Sable was awake and looking at Leanne, her forehead wrinkled in concern. She began whimpering.

"That's okay, Sable," she said, her voice rising as if speaking to a child. "I'm just popping out. I'll be back." She gave Sable a gentle stroke on the head. Satisfied, Sable readjusted herself and went back to sleep.

"I'm worried about you," Mark said. "This sounds like really bad news."

"It is. I'm sorry, Mark, but I have to go." She gave him a peck on the cheek, grabbed her jacket and bag, and left.

"Well, Sable, I guess it's just you and me again." Mark knew what was on her phone. Her parents were dead.

Chapter Nine

DISSENT
Spain

"They are beginning to talk," Fred said

"About what?" Tim asked.

"That none of their friends have contacted them and that our mission has been thwarted by the bombers. It won't take long before they put one and one together to realise that they were the bombers."

"Let them. They're contained."

"But the staff isn't. That's our weak link. The cleaners, the massage therapists, the cooks. They hear the grumbling. They're not stupid."

"So what do you propose we do?" Tim asked.

"Kill them all," Fred said.

Tim just about spilled his orange juice. "Fred, that's insane."

"No more insane than sending them to their deaths."

"One has purpose, the other is senseless."

"Selfish, not senseless," said Fred.

"Possibly, but I don't think it can be contained. First, no one suspects a bunch of old farts like us doing anything. Second, killing people with external connections like the cleaners will put the spotlight on us. And third, it's not my style."

"Then we've signed our death warrants."

"What do you think we were doing when we embarked on this?"

"I expected to be one of the bombers, not to be tortured at the hands of the Americans or Russians or, god forbid, the Chinese."

"Everything is going to plan," Tim said. "We've achieved an extraordinary victory for our cause. It is more than any military has achieved in any one stroke except for, possibly, the dropping of the bombs in Hiroshima and Nagasaki."

"Those helped speed up the end of the war in the Pacific theatre. We have just pissed off every dictator and armed power on the planet. We have likely sown the seeds for a massive global war as the powers commit to a collective letting of blood as a solution to their impotency."

"Exactly, but wrong conclusion," said Tim. "They *are* feeling impotent. Why? Because none of them caused this and they can't comprehend not knowing who is capable of this type of action. We have their undivided attention. Now we just need to deliver our message and a warning to lift the boot from our collective neck or feel this again repeatedly until they do. It won't just come from us; there will be others. They will see the manner in which they can strike. We will be their inspiration."

Fred looked at Tim sidelong. "I'm not sure if your plan is coming off as anticipated. Let's give it a couple of days and see where our heads are."

Tim held out his hand, Fred took it and the two embraced. *But we haven't come up with a solution to contain the talking,* Fred thought. *We're here with our heads in the sand instead of acting. Tim is losing it.*

∞

"Christianity had its Inquisition. Some of the greatest crimes against life and belief were committed in the names of God—as defined by the inquisitors. Women were deemed witches, and those who questioned were deemed heretics. Any opposition to their power met with one end: death." Professor Damien Holt looked into the audience of presidents and generals. The purpose of his speech was to put the current attacks into context historically. With every eye looking at the Middle East and Arab perpetrators, he was urging caution before action.

"When we criticise the Muslim fundamentalists, we need to remember our own collective past. They are but angry young teens in the evolution and maturation of their religions. Our concern should not be their intemperate outbursts but whether the world is a child-friendly environment. If yes, we should tolerate and nurture their development. Allow them to evolve in understanding and love. If no, we must face up to the existential danger and eliminate them." There was a murmur in the crowd. "I believe that we are not yet at the stage of killing a billion souls, but it does behove the Muslim community to take responsibility of their fellow Muslims and mature. The stakes are too high to allow uncivilised and extreme outbursts. The result would be the devolution of humankind."

Professor Holt closed his notes and looked at the stunned audience. *Too politically incorrect?* he thought. The moderator was already up, thanking him and ushering him off the stage.

It was at this moment that Chief Superintendent Barry Judd received a text to urgently return to base. They had a lead. *About fucking time*, he said to himself as he left the auditorium.

∞

"What do we have?" asked Judd still only half way through the door.

"Anonymous tip. I think it's real."

"Source?"

"Kings Cross, London. Something about a distant relative being held in a resort in Spain." Sergeant

Moxxit handed him a file with everything they had on the suspect.

"Spain? I can't do anything with Spain. They'll fuck the whole fucking thing up. Get me Special Branch and the prime minister. I think it's time we took some action."

"Yes sir," Moxxit said. "Time?"

"Right fucking now if you please," said Judd. He went into his office and closed the door. He had some calls of his own to make.

∞

Frederik felt terrible about his betrayal of Tim. He thought he had it in him. He had felt like killing himself prior to meeting Tim. His life really had no meaning, but this whole venture made him feel alive again. Relevant. He enjoyed the intricacies of the logistics and tension as the months turned to weeks, which turned to days, hours, minutes, and then time zero. He knew that many of the flights originated from Heathrow and the UK would be prepared to break any rules necessary to get their man—and get the credit for finding him. *I can't believe how much I want to live*, he thought. *I've become little more than a rat with a conscience.*

As Fred passed through the airport security, he replayed his anonymous conversation on the phone in his mind. He knew he was damning the others but all he could think about was saving himself.

"Hello, yes. I'd like to speak to someone about the recent bombings. Ah, yes, the plane bombings. What? No. Just information. My name? Uh, do I need to give it? I'm in enough danger as it is by calling you. Fine. Salvatore. Ignati Salvatore. Yes, I'm calling from Spain. I can't talk. He may come in at any moment. Details? People are the bombs. He detonates everything on a timer. Everyone is a bomb. No guns required. No, I haven't been drinking. No, I can't tell you any more. Address? Mine? Oh yes, it is the medical retreat just outside of Ronda in Andalucía, Spain. Name? I told you. Ah, yes. His name's Timothy Bull. He's running the show. Me? Nobody. Just another cog in the machine. Okay, I'm hanging up. No, I don't have a number. No, I don't have an email. Okay, goodbye. I gotta go. Bye, bye. Bye." Fred had hung up the payphone and wanted to vomit. He had never betrayed anyone before. His whole body was sweaty. *You're a dead man if you don't do this*, he said to himself. *You're dead anyway*, the same voice replied.

The deed done, Fred handed his boarding pass to the stewardess and walked to the plane. He had no luggage except a laptop and day bag. His destination could have been anywhere. Should have been anywhere. Instead, he chose Denmark. *Nice, boring, and safe*, he told himself.

As Fred boarded, Chief Superintendent Judd was paged in London. It was the only clue anyone in the world had to go on. Judd decided to follow it.

Fred reasoned that he himself wouldn't be suspected—unless Tim talked. And if there was one thing Fred could count on, it was Tim's silence and loyalty.

Chapter Ten

THE INTERVIEW
Spain

Near the bottom of Spain, just above the point where Europe kisses Africa, Tim found a complex of villas set on 280 hectares. It constituted a former hotel with two hundred rooms, forty-eight villas with at least five bedrooms each, and a number of smaller cottages to house service staff. He made his guests share the hotel rooms and bedrooms within the complex. Even with this economising, he was only able to house 1,280 geriatrics. After the mission, he was left with just over five hundred guests.

Set in Andalucía, one of Spain's more rugged provinces in the south, Tim's complex represented one of the best financial deals of his career. Near the famous city of Ronda, he and his guests could enjoy the rustic views of Hemmingway's famous novel or visit the bullring where the beasts would be killed in a spectacle perfected two centuries ago. The blood sport was transformed from an awkward public execution into an art form with skills in its own right. It was in Ronda that the use of a diversionary cape called a muleta and a killing sword were adopted.

"When do we arrive?" Judd asked.

"We land in Seville in forty-five minutes. We'll be met by a contingent of SAS stationed in Gibraltar. We converge in Ronda two hours later." Sergeant Moxxit was crisp and professional. He had also spent time with the Special Branch prior to being transferred to the Met.

"Any trouble from ATLAS or GEO?" Judd asked. He was relishing getting back into action. He may be old but he still had some life left in him. Met or not, he was SAS at heart.

ATLAS was formed by the European Union post 9/11 with the goal to empower co-operation among police units across the EU's twenty-eight states. The GEO was the Spanish Special Forces (Grupo Especial de Operaciones), which was small in number (fewer than 150 members) but on par with the UK's SAS or SBS. The GEO specialised in counter-terrorism and hostage situations.

"No problems yet, sir," Moxxit said.

"Have we alerted the Americans?"

"Affirmative. They're going apeshit. They want the collar."

Judd grinned. "I can imagine. Those fuckers'll have to take a back seat this time. This collar is being claimed on behalf of His Majesty the King."

"I'd love to be the one to see their faces, sir."

"Me too," Judd said. His smile stayed on his lips. "How much longer before this fucker lands?"

By the time the UK contingent arrived, the GEO had secured the area and was vacating homes and stragglers within a five mile radius of the target compound. Their work was made both easy and difficult by the terrain. Easy because there were only a couple of real roads to blockade, hard because the rest of the terrain was almost impassable by vehicle. Foot or flight only. The dull distant thud of helicopters held sentry positions on all access and exit routes within the fifteen kilometre exclusion zone. No one was going to make the mistake of underestimating the bombers.

"Who's in charge here?" Judd asked. He left the door open to the Range Rover as he started talking. The dust rose and settled on him and inside his ride.

"I am, sir."

"And you are?"

"Commander Romero Javier, GEO."

"Colonel Judd, SAS, on secondment to the Met. We lost a lot of lives on our watch."

"So did we," said Javier. "And this is Spain. This is our collar."

"I don't want any trouble," Judd said. "You can take control of the perimeter; contain the area and storm the compound if necessary. I just want our men with yours when we breach, and I want to be the negotiator."

"We're trained for this," said Javier. "It's our call."

"True," said Judd. He was on his best behaviour. "But this is my lead. Sourced from MI5 Intel. I need to be part of this."

Javier looked dubious. Judd was an old man. Negotiators had to deal with stress that would give a donkey a stroke. "What about the Americans?"

Judd grinned. "The sooner we agree on our shit, the fewer Americans we need to tolerate. They'll just create a royal clusterfuck out of a simple and contained situation."

"Glad to hear you think this is simple," Javier said. He was starting to like Judd.

"Simple like this: anyone moves within the exclusion zone, kill 'em. We're not in an urban environment. Few innocents are at risk. Hell, we could probably detonate a nuke here without too much resistance."

"Okay, I get your point. Have you ever negotiated a hostage position before?"

"Who's to say they're hostages? We believe the ring leader is there. We know he had accomplices—at least 763 of them. Who's to say the people with him aren't the same?"

"Thermal imaging shows close to five hundred people gathered in one building. Looks like the conference room of the hotel."

"That's good news for us," said Judd.

"We can put our men into position around the hotel and restrict their movements to that one building. We'll sweep the individual villas and secure the area." Javier had an aerial photo and was showing Judd the positions. Judd nodded as the plan was laid out.

"Sounds good to me. Good luck, sir. I'll create a base for myself near the entrance of the hotel. We'll make contact with him then."

∞

"How're we all feeling?" Tim said into the microphone. He was on an elevated platform that acted as a stage. His guests had gathered for an inspirational talk about life and meaning and how their actions would help all elderly around the world.

"What happened to the others?" A voice called out from the audience. There were murmurs of agreement and nodding of heads.

Tim cleared his throat and took a drink of water. "As you know, many died on that fateful day…"

"*All* died," the same voice said. "That can't be a coincidence."

"From my understanding, some survived. We are still waiting to hear from them." Tim didn't like this agitator.

"Bullshit. They're all dead. None of us have heard anything. It's been long enough by now. We should know."

Tim was about to reply when he was cut short by something else. A bull horn outside. The audience turned as one to find the sound.

"This is the police. You are surrounded." This was repeated in Arabic, Spanish, and French.

The auditorium was dead quiet. Tim moved closer to the microphone. "Calm down. I'm sure there's an easy explanation." *Shit*, he thought. *Too soon.*

There is a moment when the predator turns into prey, and another when he realises it. At that moment, Tim felt the jaws of the cat around his mouse-like existence. He had felt like a tiger, but was now a mouse. He hadn't planned for this. No one could know about him. *Maybe they were mistaken*, he thought.

"You are surrounded. Come out with your hands where we can see them."

The phone rang next to a lectern standing near the entrance to the auditorium. A member of the crowd answered it, was silent, and then held it up towards Tim. "I think it's for you," she said.

Tim made his way to her and gently took the handset in his right hand. "Hello?" he said.

"Mr. Timothy Bull?" a voice said.

"Yes."

"This is Commander Romero Javier of the Grupo Especial de Operaciones. We have information that leads us to believe you're involved with the recent bombings. We may be mistaken. We just want to talk."

Tim's heart was beating fast. He wasn't shaking but his pulse felt like a drum. "I'm not sure what you are talking about," Tim said. "We're a group of elderly citizens living out our lives the best we can."

"Then you won't mind us talking to you."

Tim went silent.

"Are you there?" said Javier.

Tim couldn't bring himself to say the words. He thought of himself as a champion of his age and class. Now he felt like some cheap stupid terrorist. *Maybe that's all I've become,* he thought.

He hung up the phone without responding. It wasn't long before it rang again.

"We seem to have been disconnected," Javier said. "What would you like to do, Mr. Bull?"

"Please, call me Tim."

"Okay Tim, what would you like to do?"

"I don't know, sir," Tim said. "Right now, I don't know what's going on."

"Perhaps we could send someone in to talk to you?"

Tim paused. He knew these situations never ended well, usually with some team of crack troops shooting the bad guys. Then he realised it. *They don't know if we are bad guys,* he thought.

"That sounds reasonable. No tricks please." *At least it'll buy me some time to think.*

Within a few minutes, there was a knock on the hotel's front door. One of the guests answered it. His movements were slow and deliberate. He was eighty-two and still able to get around, but the age took its toll. The other members had been using the toilets, getting coffee, and enjoying the buffet of food and snacks laid out for the planned talk that day. *All in all, they are behaving like pros*, thought Tim, *despite the odd agitator. And even he has gone quite.*

When Judd walked in, all eyes turned to him. They saw a well-dressed Englishman—the suit-sense and pale skin was unmistakable—enter the room. Judd saw an entire auditorium stuffed with ancient people. Walking frames, canes, and the slow motion movement of people terrified of falling lest they break a hip or limb. He took a moment to take it all in. *There are no terrorist leaders in here*, he thought. *Just victims.*

"I'm looking for Timothy Bull," he said in a loud voice.

The eyes betrayed them. They turned to look at Tim. Realising the futility of a ruse, he stepped forward. "Here, sir."

"Hello. It looks like we have a situation, Mr. Bull. I'm here to talk and see if we can work through this before anyone gets hurt. I'm with the British Security Forces. I hope you don't mind having a word with me." It was a statement, not a request.

Judd made his way to Tim, his senses taking in potential threats. He couldn't see any. Just decrepit old people. *What the fuck's going on?* he thought. Outwardly, he was all smiles as he extended his hand to Tim. Inwardly, red flags were waving.

"Hello sir, please call me Tim." He shook Judd's hand.

"Okay Tim, call me Barry." As he said it, Judd shuddered. *Maybe I'm not cut out for this shit,* he thought. "First, Tim, I can see there are a lot of people here, many of whom look quite frail. Any chance we could get a list of who's here and maybe discuss letting some go while we continue our conversation?"

"That seems right to the point," Tim said. "Aren't you supposed to befriend me, make me feel safe, and *then* make that type of request?"

"Frankly, they don't look like they'll make it if I talk too long."

It may not have been meant as a joke, but Tim laughed. "I like that, Barry. Funny. Okay, I'm happy for anyone who needs assistance to walk to leave." Tim turned to the guests and used the microphone. "Listen up everyone. Anyone who wants to leave can leave now. There are officers outside who will assist you. If you want to stay, please stay. I'm not forcing you."

What the fuck? Judd's mind was going into over-drive. *Were we mistaken? Do we have the wrong guy? He doesn't look like much, but at least he's the leader.*

"Nicola," Tim continued. "For those who wish to stay, please take their details like name and physical condition. The police would like to know who to help."

A plump woman with a permanent smile on her face stepped forward and took charge of that activity. So far, the guests were enjoying the change of routine. There was the constant shuffle to and from the toilets and coffee machines but no one left. Judd tried to take it all in.

For Tim's part, he was trying to determine where Fred disappeared to. *His absence speaks volumes*, he thought.

"Thank you for that," Judd said. "From my perspective, I don't know why we're here. But obviously there has been some intelligence gathered that is pointing to you. Do you want to talk about it?"

Tim could think of nothing else. He had prepared himself for this moment but he didn't expect it to arrive so soon. He was pleased he at least had a forum for his message.

"Yes, Barry, I think we can talk. But I'd like to ask you for something first."

"Shoot." Judd kicked himself. *What fucking moron says 'shoot' to a possible terrorist?*

"Funny," Tim said. "I'd like to ensure no one gets hurt. None of these people here are guilty of anything other than being old and in need of some sun and care. As you can see around you, we try to keep them comfortable."

Judd agreed. "Anything else?"

"I'd like to have three network stations here to do a live interview. It should be the BBC, Al Jazeera, and China Daily."

Judd paused. "I'll have to get back to you on that." He pulse spiked while trying to remain outwardly calm. *This fucker's guilty*, he thought. *I just can't believe it. Who asks for a live interview if they weren't?*

"Perhaps we reconvene when you're able to confirm," Tim said.

"Fair enough. I will call when ready. If you need to contact us, just pick up the phone. It's always on and connected only to us."

With that, the two shook hands and Judd left.

∞

"You wouldn't fucking believe it," Judd said. "I still don't believe it and I fucking saw it. They are all either guilty as sin or none of them are. I don't think any of them are hostages. Or, if they are, they don't care. It's like he has them in a spell of some sort."

"Drugs? Are they conscious?" Javier asked.

"It's not that. They're just old. Everyone's ancient. One-foot-in-the-grave-old." Judd was trying to make sense of what he had seen. "If I had certainty of guilt, I would kill 'em all. As it stands, we have secured the theatre of operations and have the option of taking our time."

"What about their request for live TV?" Javier said.

"I think we should give it to them. At least there'll be an interview instead of one of those Jihad videos the Arab nutters do."

"Are they Arabs? Muslims? Africans?"

"White as the driven snow," Judd said. "These are the least likely terrorists I have ever seen. More likely for them to be your local Santa Clause than Satan. That's what bothers me the most. If we're wrong and kill them all, we will have just committed the largest mass killing of European citizens outside of wartime."

"And we'll be facing court martial and jail time."

"Or worse."

"Instead of being hailed as heroes the rest of our lives." Javier turned and took a piece of paper from an aide. "BBC is already here, along with SKY and Al Jazeera. No China press here yet." Only Javier and Judd spoke.

"Let's see if that's good enough for this fucker," Judd said. He picked up the phone, had a short conversation, and hung up. "We're in. Call the reporters. Get three TVs with real feeds. This guy wants to watch himself live as he broadcasts. He feels we may trick him otherwise."

"Smart guy," Javier said. "Sure we shouldn't just kill him and silence him now?"

"I think the world wants closure. They want conclusive proof that these people did it. My PM instructed me on this. Personally, I'd riddle the whole lot of them with bullets. Fuck 'em. Let God sort 'em out."

∞

"This is BBC...", "This is SKY ...", "This is Al Jazeera,"—"...broadcasting to you LIVE from near Ronda in the south of Spain. If you have just joined us, we have breaking news on the recent plane bombings.

We will be interviewing the alleged leader of the until-now unknown group who may have been behind the bombings.

"One moment, here he is. For the audience at home, the person we are interviewing has requested live transmissions from the global networks. There is no seven second delay and we can only caution you that there may be inappropriate language."

"Good afternoon and thank you for joining me here today. My name is Timothy Bell and we are sitting with almost five hundred of my guests of this resort with you, the world. I wanted to have a chance to say my piece without the torture or other due processes awaiting me. Just so you know, there are armed anti-terrorist military and police services surrounding the complex as well as extensive secondary and tertiary measures in place. I am otherwise under no duress. I have no delusions about how this ends for me. I am here to set the record straight."

The BBC reporter asked, "John Hill of BBC News. I would like to ask the question the world would like to know. Did you do it and why?"

"That's what I like," Tim said smiling. "A direct question. No messing around."

The reporters didn't crack a smile. Nor did Judd or the troops outside. Nor did the billion plus people watching the feed via their televisions, mobiles, or computers. The whole world held their collective breath.

Tim, for his part, watched the monitor and his mobile. One of his conditions was for the network not to have the seven second delay between what he said and transmission. He was satisfied this was being complied with.

"Yes, I caused this to be done."

The reporters collectively and instinctively smelled blood. This was like being able to interview Hitler or Bin Laden. *And he admitted it*, they all thought. The police felt a shock of human electricity run through them all. Guns were gripped more firmly, sights became clearer, and everyone's resolve strengthened. Politicians could feel the victory lap. And without any casualties. Very civilised.

"I did it as a message to the world. We are the normal people. The safe people. The people who work every day of their lives, pay their taxes, walk when the signs say walk, and stop when they say stop. We follow the rules. We make our countries great. But you don't know when to stop. You take more and more taxes. We can live with that if you spent it wisely and honestly. You distrust us more each day—ostensibly for security—but it comes down to money. You trace our honest pennies while the thieves count their stolen dollars; the crooks crook. You listen to our calls and read our mail under the pretence of security. You war and allow others to war on each other, increasing the threats to peace. And you sell arms to make the world continue to war on each other. You talk as though there is an 'us and them', making the Arabs the enemy. Then you excuse their violence as an outburst of Muslim pride and consequence to our poor behaviour towards them. This is bullshit. Stop selling or giving them weapons. Treat them as enemies when they act like enemies and decide that you want to win.

"In the last sixty years, the world has forgotten how to win a war. It has always settled. A truce is called, only to see a further eruption later. The world doesn't understand these shade of grey. They understand winners and losers. Bureaucrats and administrators understand grey.

"Our act of education was a wakeup call—to the powers of the world, to the people of the world—that you don't need to put up with the oppression we currently live with."

The Al Jazeera reporter asked, "Rizwan Omaar of Al Jazeera, reporting live. Please tell me, Mr. Bull, how would you solve these problems? If it was easy, it would have been done by now, wouldn't it?"

"I would make the sale of arms a war crime. If your country can't make arms, you don't get them. That would be my single most important rule. If you need help, invite a friendly army into your territory to protect you. No sane ruler would do this. And the war crime is tied to the manufacturer and the politicians. Unless and until we make our producers of death responsible, this will continue.

"But you will find resistance to this from the US, Britain, Germany, France, Russia, China, and others. It's big business. What I'm saying today is that it's not big enough business when you look at the consequences. Prior to the introduction of the concept of duty of care with the creation of the tort of negligence, we couldn't sue manufactures nor producers of defective goods. Whether this is a mouse in a ginger beer or a faulty wiring system in your car, the producer now has a duty of care to the public. All I say is that we should expand this to arms. If a country wants its citizens to be armed, great. The US constitution guarantees it. But it doesn't mean for it to then arm or bolster global conflicts.

"We have a United Nations and we recognise war crimes. Well, except the US, which has opted out. We may need a special category for arms sales. I initially thought to allow an exception for police calibre trade but even this should be banned. Nuclear war and attack helicopters and tanks are scary enough, but most people die from small arms."

The Sky reporter said, "Donna Sykes of Sky News. You say this can be done, but it sounds to me like you are a kid having a tantrum and forcing the parents to give him some toys."

"All I am saying is that we need to go to war and determine who wins or loses, or we de-escalate the violence. The violence begets the security needs, which beget erosion of freedoms, which beget a repressed and angry populace. I am trying to create peace."

"Like fucking for virginity," Judd said to himself. He had heard enough of the bullshit. He felt his phone vibrate: urgent message from the PM. He decided to step outside to take the call and have a cigarette. Being around all those old folks was freaking him out. The whole idea grated with his sense of right and wrong.

He reached the command post and found Javier with a coffee and cigarette. He got a fresh coffee and bummed a smoke. It felt good to rest his bones as he sat next to Javier. He could feel the muscles relax in his lower back. His shoulders dropped slightly. Judd leaned back in his chair to enjoy his cigarette as he began dialling a number on the secure phone line. At that precise moment, the entire building in front of them exploded in a ball of fire.

Judd's body lunged forward and off his chair. He dropped what was in his hands and went running towards the blast.

"I thought you said the complex was safe," yelled Javier, also running, one step behind Judd.

"I did. Nothing. No suicide belts, no guns, nothing. Just a buffet with snacks on it." Judd went white. *All on live fucking* TV, he thought.

∞

What happened would become fodder for much debate. Everyone saw the septuagenarian talking calmly to the three reporters. The cameras were focused on him but each network had two further cameras, one to show the interviewer and one to show the five hundred or so guests and their surroundings. Most people were in light cotton shirts, flip-flops, and sweat pants.

In between Tim and the reporters was a table replete with coffee, juices, water, and some Danish pastries. Tim ensured a serrated steak knife was there to cut the food if necessary.

"So you are saying," said the BBC reporter, "you managed to kill 276,822 people on 763 planes and cause a global crisis with little more than the will to do so?"

"Yes. The people who ultimately sacrificed themselves were unaware of their role. I want to make that clear. I alone am to blame for this." Tim could see the disquiet amongst the guests. He had now just answered their question of earlier that day. Murmurs began to ripple throughout the auditorium.

"Forgive me for saying this," continued the same reporter, "but how could you have done this? You look more like my uncle than a terrorist."

"The will of a person is not determined by their skin colour or religion. Until now, we only looked for terrorists among Muslims from the Middle East and Africa. Some condoned their violence as a consequence of our oppression. I wonder if the world will do the same when they digest our acts of patriotism." Tim was drifting in his thoughts. "As you can see, we are all white, affluent, Northern Europeans of no discernible religious affiliation. Your bombers were discarded carcasses, left to rot and die by the state. I chose those without families, and we became their families. We genuinely helped them and gave their lives purpose—even if unwittingly on their part."

"Excuse me for interrupting," said the Al Jazeera reporter, "but how did you manage it? With all due respect, it is impossible for you to have done what you claim to have done without outside help. Which government or militia did this for you?"

"You aren't hearing me," Tim said. He sighed. "I guess our message has been sent. Those who will hear will hear. The rest of you, well, let me show you instead."

Tim took a sip of water. His mouth had gone dry in anticipation. He took the steak knife and, without warning, stabbed it into his abdomen at just the right angle to pierce the two membranes separating the deadly liquids inside him.

The blast was instant. Tim was incinerated, as were the reporters immediately next to him. By the time the blast hit the first row of the audience, its force had dissipated sufficiently from incineration to merely explosive force. The first row was obliterated into flesh and bits of bone. The second row received the blast sufficiently diminished to allow the liquids within their abdomen to rupture and mix, causing a further blast. Every five rows back, roughly, the audience became bombs. All and everybody else was incinerated or blasted into tiny pieces of liquefied flesh.

There was barely a gap between explosions. For the viewers around the world, the feed was cut. They would mutter conspiracy and cover up, but the truth was simple. There were no more reporters or cameras. The feed changed abruptly to those outside of the building. At the time, they were interviewing police and members of the services willing to oblige. Prior to the interview, they had drawn the short straw and had mumbled about loss of career opportunities. Now they were alive and on the front line. It was Sky News that best captured the plume of the explosives coming from the former medical hotel.

Chapter Eleven

CONSEQUENCES

What followed was an uproar of talking heads, military posturing, and the call by politicians to publish all arms dealers and anyone capable of supplying materials capable of replicating those body bombs. All doctors were deemed a security risk and any veterinarian, nurse, or staff who had any surgical knowledge were forced to register in the global registry of persons of interest. The choice was simple: register or be fired and be banned from practicing their profession. They registered. The administrators and security experts were determined to quantify and contain the risk of these types of attacks and prevent them from ever happening again.

Some talked of banning books or internet links that might teach readers how to conduct surgical procedures. Even surgical instruments became monitored and tracked; eventually, more so than guns.

In the days and weeks following the interview, newspapers competed in the publishing of the world's evils. It was as though they wanted to exculpate themselves of responsibility. Arms dealers were reported on, complete with pictures and brief biographies. Drug dealers and financiers were set out next to each other as contributors to the world's instability. It was a brief period of transparency, but normality would return soon enough. No society could function in a state of constant hysterics. People would become numbed to the new reality.

∞

One person who wouldn't become numb was Jack Harding. His biological father killed his parents in front of him before committing suicide. Jack only found out later; for most of his life, he thought his biological father was just a kindly old man who lived two doors down from him. He was wrong about his parents and the man who killed them. They were deep cover CIA, investigating an even more secretive group trying to create a single global currency. Jack was drawn in due to a different department of the CIA's learning of the plot. Time would tell whether Jack or the deaths of his parents had any effect on that conspiracy. But after that, he was marked for death.

To stay alive, he changed his identity. The old man, while turning out to be the biggest bastard alive, left him a fortune and the tools to stay alive. In a macabre twist, Jack took the old man's last name. That was almost a decade ago. He was on the run but slowly his fear turned to hatred. He wanted to strike back at the world that so devastated his. He met Timothy Bull and the two began to talk. The inspiration and strategy for what happened on 25 June, 2025, was born shortly after that meeting.

"Another, sir?" The waiter was young, probably a university student earning some extra cash between classes.

"No thank you. Just the bill please." Jack was finishing his breakfast of German white sausage with mustard and a tall glass of wheat beer. It was an acquired taste. The heavy sourdough bread helped it go down and he still chased it all with a strong black coffee with a glass of water on the side.

The Bavarian themed café was not too far from the Brandenburg Gate and what remained of the famed wall that divided Berlin all those years ago. Jack enjoyed the energy of Berlin and was contemplating going east. It was the interview that changed his mind. He recognised betrayal when he saw it. There was only one person who knew the details and who wasn't on the video footage that day: Fredrick Johansen. *I'm still alive because Tim didn't tell Fred about me*, he thought. *I think I'll return the favour by thanking Fred in person.*

He knew about Fred, now he just had to find him. He needed to call in some favours from some friends he met along the way. One of the benefits of being on the run from the world's largest intelligence gatherers is that you learn some intelligence gathering tricks of your own. If you didn't, you didn't stay alive.

∞

Love is something experienced, as in the way in which a sailor overboard clings to a raft or piece of driftwood. It is a zone in which a few lucky people live. It can't be manufactured or relived at will. A drowning man is different from a man swimming for leisure. In one case, the driftwood means life; the other, a distraction. If one is honest, who amongst us lives in that zone? When you cross your threshold, your dog is so happy it can jump out of its skin. Do you feel that when your lover enters the room? Or her you? Do we live in a mirage, in constant denial, hoping to grasp that moment when love was real?

Mark put down his pen, his diary open. The bottle of scotch was half drunk and Sable, content, slept at his feet. "I was loved once," Mark said to her. "I was the fool who didn't know how to love back. If I'm given another chance, I won't make that mistake." Sable looked up at him, acknowledging his earnestness and waiting to see if food was coming or maybe some solid scratching or rubbing. She loved to have her ear scratched, her body rubbed, and the gentle hands of her master patting her saying that everything was okay. She waited and then put her muzzle between her paws.

Her eyes remained open, waiting for any more discussion from her master, but then slowly began to droop. It wasn't long before her breathing returned to the slow and steady rhythm of sleep.

Mark abandoned his thoughts and made his way to the sofa. It wasn't far. The open plan kitchen could have allowed him to watch the television from the kitchen table but the sofa was more comfortable. He settled into it and put the scotch on the floor where his arm flopped. He had no intention of moving from this spot until he woke up the next morning. Sable followed and, after waiting for permission, put one foot on the sofa. Noticing no objection, she jumped on. Seeing her master move slightly to allow her room, she circled twice and then slept up against Mark. He liked the physical contact and he knew he was making a mistake. He'd never get her to stay off the sofa now. He didn't care. He clicked on the power and waited for the television to warm up. It took a couple of seconds but already he was impatiently flipping through the stations. Finding nothing he liked, he settled on a wildlife show. Something about the rain forest and the creatures that co-existed seemed strangely calming and reassuring.

He wasn't a big drinker, but he liked the slow, steady burn of good scotch or aged rum in the quiet of an evening. It was a distraction and generally caused him to wake up in the middle of the night, but it passed the time. And time was moving slowly since Leanne left in such a hurry. He couldn't blame her; he had seen the texts. But it had been three days and he hadn't heard from her. He didn't presume anything as grand as love, but he didn't dismiss it. There was something about her for him, and him for her. *This is crazy*, he thought. *I spent months after waking from the coma all alone, and yet these three days seem longer.*

Sable's head popped up and her head tilted to one side, ears forward. Then she got up and ran to the door, whimpering.

"What's up Sable? Who's there? Do you need to go out?"

Mark got up and went to the patio door and slid it open. The rain was falling gently and he really didn't fancy the smell of wet dog.

It was the knock on the door that brought him back into the present. Sable was wagging her body and started to tremble with excitement. She wanted to bark and keep quiet at the same time. Mark was happy she wasn't a yappy dog.

When he opened the door, Sable bolted and jumped up at the wet figure. Her hair was wet and clothes soaked. She barely acknowledged Sable and was looking straight at Mark.

"I'm sorry I didn't call," Leanne said.

"You never need to apologise to me," he said. He stepped back and let her in.

"I just needed some time. My parents… my parents died and I haven't been coping too well."

"You don't need to explain. I'm just glad to see you." He opened his arms and she put herself against him. Sable was running around them, half-jumping to try to join the hug.

"Do you mind if I stay here tonight? I can't be alone."

Mark kissed her and led her to the bedroom to get some dry clothes. "I'll be in the kitchen making coffee."

"I'd prefer what you're already drinking," she said.

"A girl after my own heart," he said. "I'll see you on the sofa. You'd better hurry. Sable has learned that I'm a marshmallow in the discipline department. She might take your spot."

"Don't worry, I'll find a place," she said with a smile. "And Mark?"

"Yeah?"

"Thanks."

"For what?"

"For this."

∞

The next morning, Mark's world was full of possibilities. Where before there was darkness and gloom, now all he could see was sunlight and hope. The coffee never smelt better, the toast was exceptionally tasty, and the salted butter melted just the way he liked it. He let Leanne sleep. *She must not be a morning person*, he thought. He enjoyed this part of the day the most. He boiled an egg, just in case she wanted one, and waited for her to wake up as he drank his second cup.

Half way through it, he made his way outside and got the newspaper. It was wrapped in plastic and placed perfectly in front of his door. He enjoyed the physical sense of a newspaper. The ink, the paper, the temporary nature of it all. Even the reckless environmental impact of papers appealed to him. Computers and online news never felt the same. It seemed more real in paper. It was tangible. He couldn't figure it out but he did know what he liked. It seemed civilised to read one's paper in the morning with your coffee.

He separated the sports and home sections and put them aside. He enjoyed the front section and the business section, even though he barely had two cents to rub together. He lived vicariously through the lives of the people in print. This scandal, that leveraged buyout, another crisis. He wasn't a tabloid reader but sometimes even the most staid newspapers seemed like celebrity rubbish.

The front page was full of the dramatic Spanish bust (and boom, to quote the paper). Pictures of the victims and the heroes of the arrest were displayed prominently. This continued with a promised special edition on the weekend setting out all the inside details of the arrest and the lunatics who perpetrated the crime. *Bizarre*, thought Mark. *Reality is stranger than fiction.*

He turned to page 8, which had the obituary of Leanne's parents. They were wealthier and more important than he thought. As he read, he felt the cold fingers of anxiety creep up his legs and into his chest. He put down the paper. He didn't want to know any more.

"Morning, sweetheart," Leanne said. She was wearing one of his shirts. It stopped just past her bum and the front was a little higher. Mark couldn't believe that she was in the same apartment as him. She was really out of his league.

"I hope you slept okay. I made some toast." He got up to make some fresh coffee and got a serious kiss from her as he passed. Just her touch got his innards going. She really did something to him.

"Slept like a baby. Hi Sable. Miss me?" Sable body-wagged and she went to the patio door to be let out. Leanne opened the door and left it open. The morning air was cool but not cold. Neither of them noticed it.

When she saw the paper opened to her parents' obituary, she became silent.

"I'm sorry. I was just reading the paper and reached that section when you came in."

"No need to be sorry. Did you read the entire article?"

"No. Most. I'm really sorry."

"It's me who is sorry. Do you still want me to be here?" Leanne slumped in her chair, all sexiness and happiness gone.

"What? Are you crazy? Why? I'm a little intimidated by your wealth but I don't want you to leave."

"So you haven't read the whole article." She stopped and picked up the paper. "I expect it would be an expose of the family's dirty secrets. I just found out myself. It was one of the reasons I almost didn't come back. I was too ashamed."

Mark came next to Leanne and put his arm around her. "I don't know what you're talking about. All I read was that they were rich and powerful and would be missed and that you are the sole successor and now CEO of quite a big organisation. I first thing I thought of was that you were out of my league and why you were even with me. I don't have anything to offer you." It was his turn to be deflated.

"You have everything to offer me. You actually like me for me. That's all I ever wanted. What more can any of us offer each other?"

"Are you serious? You are so beautiful, so sexy, so smart, so… everything. I can see myself falling in love with you if I'm not careful."

"Then let's not be careful." She put the paper aside and kissed him. She led him to the bedroom. The coffee could wait.

Sable found her way into the bedroom later that morning. The two of them were lying in each other's arms, asleep. It was a cold nose that Leanne felt on her feet that tickled her awake.

"I think we forgot to feed Sable."

"She always has food. She's just being a pain in the ass," Mark said.

She laughed lightly and got up. "Don't you want to know what I was so afraid of you knowing?"

"Not really. None of my business. If you wanted me to know, you'd tell me. I'm happy with the Leanne I met and am getting to know. We are only what we are, not what others say we are."

"Wow, profound so early in the morning. Sex must get the juices flowing." She found a robe and put it one. "Speaking of which, I'm starving and I never got that coffee."

Mark pulled himself from bed and followed her. He wore some sweat pants and a t-shirt, which had been thrown on the floor.

When she finished her first cup, she turned to Mark. "I want to tell you."

"Okay, but only if you want to. I really don't need to know. Every family has secrets. You will probably hate me when you find out about mine."

"I think I've got you beat. My dirty secret is pretty bad. Remember when I said my parents were in trade and had consolidated their profits into prime property?"

"Yeah. Sounded pretty decent. Get some of the chips off the table. Profit taking is not a bad thing."

"No, but I only found out now what they were profiting from."

"What's that? Drugs?" Mark said it in jest.

"Worse. Arms."

Chapter Twelve

HERO

"Well done, Judd. You are a credit to your country and unit." Sir Reginald, head of MI5, lifted his glass to Judd and the two sat silently in the chief's office overlooking the Thames. "You'll probably become *Sir* Barry Judd soon enough."

"It was a disaster from the beginning to the end, Sir. We shouldn't have been so relaxed. If I put a bullet in that bastard's head, none of this would have happened." Judd couldn't get the images from his mind. He had seen a lot of action in his time. Body parts, barbarism, injustice. But seeing those helpless people blow themselves up disquieted him.

"Nonsense, my dear boy. We have a confession *and* a demonstration. No ghosts to run after. No soldiers coming back in body bags. No war to resolve this. Compare this to 9/11 and the impact it caused. We are only recovering today, almost twenty-five years later.

No, I'd say Spain was a great success, and I put a lot of the credit on your shoulders."

"You are too kind, Sir." *But we did lose good men there as well,* he thought. *Nameless men who were in position to breach at a moment's notice. I just didn't give the order.* He knew the victory was a team effort but the public needed a face to associate with the act. *Looks like I'm going to be made into a hero,* he thought.

"Not at all. The UK and the world owe you a debt of gratitude and, for my part, I'll do everything I can to make sure you receive it."

"Thank you, Sir."

"That reminds me. The powers that be are arranging for a dinner and speeches to mark the occasion. The PM and some heavy hitters will be there. You're to be there as well, I'm afraid. They will want to see and talk to you."

"Yes sir. I'll be there." *Fuck,* Judd said to himself. *Just what I need.*

∞

The dinner was held at the Dorchester Hotel, off Park Lane, in London. The ballroom was huge. Ever since the interview, security forces were at a loss as to how to determine risk. They decided they couldn't do much about it and tasked others to figure it out sooner than later. In the interim, they resorted to Israeli security tactics. They looked at every person. They profiled risk and dealt with each person as a potential threat. It slowed things down but everyone understood and submitted willingly.

"Harry, glad to see you could make it." Jason's father didn't always call his old friend Sir.

"Ah yes, Jim, wouldn't miss it. Hello Jason. Nice to see you again. Big day, what?" Harry was three drinks in and feeling good. He had a beautiful girl on his arm who was half his age.

"Evening Sir Harry. Yes, should be a cracker. I hear the SAS or Met guy who tracked down the bomber is here. I was going to ask you. Is it legal for the SAS to be acting as a Met officer? I heard a rumour that he was actually with MI5."

"No questions please," Harry laughed. "I'm no longer in office. I'll check on it though. I have a feeling more people are going to ask this." With that, Sir Harry and his date mingled further into the crowd.

"Have you seen your mother?" Jim asked his son.

"I think she's finding our seat," Jason said.

"I'll go and join her."

As Jason's father made his way to their designated table, Jason went to find the bar. Next to it were some broad shouldered men in black ties next to the face everyone in the world now knew. Jason went to meet him.

"Hello, sir. I just wanted to shake your hand. You're a real live hero."

Judd was flush from alcohol and compliments. "Thank you. Just doing my job."

"Well, I wanted to thank you for it." Jason was sincere.

"Now if only I could find that sniper, my life would be complete." Judd said it and immediately regretted his loose tongue. Tonight was a celebration, not time to wallow in missed opportunities.

"Uh, yeah," Jason's mouth went dry. "Good luck with that. I don't envy the sniper with you on his trail." He wanted to get out of there fast. It was as though a cowl of cold had smothered the gaiety from the moment. He nodded at Judd and left without ordering a drink.

Strange, thought Judd. He felt a tingle of something. A nibble. A lead? *More likely I just need to take a piss.*

The rest of the evening went well. Dinner was okay, nothing special. The tickets cost £500 per plate but it was for charity and renting the Dorchester for the event didn't come cheap.

Chapter Thirteen

The Patriot

Jeb Wall was a patriot. He believed in the constitution and thought the Federal Reserve as well as the taxes the federal government imposed on its citizens were unconstitutional. He loved America and would die for it. He had served in two tours of duty in Afghanistan. He had a small cabin in the woods away from civilisation just in case. In that cabin, he stock piled food to last him two years in preparation for the inevitable economic upheaval and social unrest that would rip his great country apart. The food was stored in sealed plastic barrels with nitrogen to enhance its preservation. He had four hunting rifles, an assault rifle, and two handguns, all with ammunition. He had a compound bow and all the fishing gear necessary to live off the land. While he was trained to live with just a knife and his wits, he wanted to have an easier go at it when the time came.

Jeb's job was as a security officer for a large food wholesaler, where he worked the night shift. He liked this because it kept his days free. He hadn't slept well anyway—not since Kabul.

During his many hours doing nothing, he would surf the net and read whatever was going on in the world. It was during one of these sessions that he came across Jason's revolutionary creed along with the video of the assassinations. He found himself nodding as the bodies fell and the words followed. *This guy's a genius*, he said to himself.

He read the obituary of Leanne's family with little interest. It simply followed from the more interesting news of the global bombers. *I can't believe they weren't Ay-rabs*, he thought as he looked at the pictures of the confessed terrorists. It was the end of the obituary that Jeb found interesting. It was a passing reference, but he was able to search the details online. *They were trading arms with the enemy. I was getting myself shot at in Kabul and other shithole places without names by weapons supplied by these assholes.* Jeb remembered the call to arms by the revolutionary video.

I'll kill that bitch and do the world a favour.

∞

"You're taking the news very well. I was bowled over and couldn't breathe. I vomited. I was too ashamed to show my face."

"I don't think you need to be ashamed at all. I'm not against guns," Mark said. "I think it's our constitutional right to bear arms. We need to protect ourselves from home invaders and foreign terrorists. I don't see it as a bad thing."

"Are you just saying that because you want to get laid again?" Leanne smiled. She was opening her robe suggestively, showing a bit of leg.

"I'd be lying if I said that wasn't a factor. But the truth of the matter is, I don't see what the problem is. Your parents sold to bad guys to kill other bad guys. Better them than us."

"Are you for real?" Leanne came closer to Mark and sat on his lap. His arm instinctively held her leg and then started tracing as far as his reach allowed.

"I try to be. Now, let's change the subject. I really have no problem with that. To be honest, your wealth is more intimidating to me than any skeletons your parents had. Do you want to take Sable for a walk? Remember, I'm also in need of walking. Did I mention I just came out of a coma?"

"Don't try to win me over with the sympathy vote," she said. "Let's go. At some point I'll need to go to the office. I'll call in and take today off. I think your rehab is more important for my health. I need to keep you fit if we're going to keep doing what we did this morning." She kissed him and walked to the bedroom. "I just need to shower and then I'm ready to go."

What did I do to deserve her? thought Mark.

Chapter Fourteen

GABRIEL AND IMBAL
Israel

Israel is full of big personalities and big egos. Each one thinks they are smart enough to be the prime minister. Each one knows better than the other. Each one thinks they are unique. This is a combination of being Jewish and the history that forged Israel. Judaism could be called the original cult of the individual. Every life is sacred and is to be protected at all costs. The wisdom of the Kabala and Talmud was influenced by the Zoroastrians but, in turn, influenced the Hellenists such as Socrates, Plato, and Aristotle. The difference was that the thread of Judaic learning was never severed, whereas the ancient Greeks were lost and saved for the West by the Arabs. As history unfolded, a persistent influence of Judaic thought permeated Western philosophy. Whether this was because Jews were educated and advised the courts or whether the philosophies of the ancients were so utterly lost is unknown. Despite being killed, persecuted, and driven from country to country, Judaism survived. Its core remained and could not but influence the fledgling European powers. Jews who were forced to convert to Christianity if they wished to serve at court didn't just lose their training or history. If there was one thing Judaism taught, it was continuity and the law. Jurisprudence, that body of legal thought in the West's legal system, is a reflection of the Judaic tradition that commenced shortly after the death of Christ—the Mishnah. The Mishnah reflected the collective Rabbinical thought that encompassed what it meant to be Jewish. Jurisprudence is the science, study, and theory of law; in essence, what it means to be law.

Whatever the reasons, Israelis are different from global Jewry. Jews may be embarrassed to say they are Jewish when confronted by hostility or even just the question, 'Where are you from?' Instead, they opt for British, American, South African, and so on. An Israeli will say he's Israeli and then look at you in the eye. If a fight ensued, he was ready for it.

When, after six decades of terrorist attacks against it, Israel decided to build a wall along its borders with the Arabs, the world was aghast. Parallels were drawn between the current Israelis and the Nazis or the Russians or the Apartheids. When the world was moving away from racial profiling, Israel was moving closer towards it. They had an idea of who their enemy was and what they looked like.

Freedoms were eroded and security became the trump card for Israelis. When an action was questioned, the point of security was raised and the question disappeared. But so did the suicide bombings and mass killings. It was a balance of life the Israelis were prepared to accept.

"Did you hear about what happened yesterday in Tel Aviv?" Gabriel was eating his breakfast of finely chopped cucumbers, tomatoes, and onions. He added some apple and cheese to it as he liked the range of tastes.

"I think so. Are you talking about the idiot who was stabbing everyone?" Imbal was getting the kids ready and trying to eat at the same time.

"I don't know where they find these guys. I'm just glad they're not smarter. Just imagine what must be going through their minds. They must know they're dead the moment they pull out the knife."

"Yeah, but this guy managed to pull that knife out while the deputy prime minister was in Jaffa and then started stabbing anyone with an open window stuck in traffic. He killed an American tourist in the process and stabbed twenty-three people, some quite badly."

"But the best part," Gabe took over from Imbal, "was how he was stopped. There was a busker doing his thing with a guitar when he saw this idiot running and stabbing everyone. There were no police, no soldiers, nothing in the area. So the guy uses his guitar and smashes it over the terrorist."

"Good for him. I didn't hear how it ended," Imbal said. She was interested but also tired at the same old stories. Just last week an eighty-year-old woman pulled a knife and stabbed a soldier in Jerusalem. Most of the stabbings were in Jerusalem lately. There were also more police and soldiers there as a result.

"It ended in typical Israeli fashion. The police arrived and shot the terrorist dead. No trial required."

"You know, when you say this to people in the world, they think we're crazy. But it's not too different than the State Troopers in the US. If someone looks hostile, they'll shoot first and ask questions later."

"Agreed," said Gabe. "But all of our terrorists get killed. It's policy. No sense imprisoning them and then releasing them to kill us."

"Well, that's Israel. The land of milk and honey and terrorists." Imbal was tired of the subject.

"I'm just glad the incidents are so few and far between now. It may not be the most politically correct system, but it works." Gabriel was finishing his salad and started walking to the sink, still chewing. "Are you coming with me or should I go by myself today?"

"I think we can make a family outing of it. Jerusalem is beautiful this time of year. Not too hot, not too cold. And I'd like to take our children to the bazaar. It's a great place."

"You're the boss. I'll get the car ready. Anything special we need to take along?"

"No. Just ourselves." Imbal kissed Gabe and packed some snacks for the one hour trip.

When they arrived, they parked near the old city's gate and walked into the chaos. The stone had a golden honey colour to it and had been there for thousands of years. Romans, Christians, Arabs, and Jews lived and walked these steps daily. It was the beauty of this stone that prompted the British administrator overseeing the city, when it was still a British asset, to make a city law requiring all new buildings to use the Jerusalem stone. As a result, today Jerusalem still looks beautiful while other cities like Tel Aviv look like concrete slums.

"Keep close to me," Imbal said, grabbing the hands of her children. She handed her son to Gabe and she held on to her daughter.

"Are you looking for anything interesting?" Gabe asked.

"Not really. I just love the chaos and nonsense of this place. It makes me think we can still live in peace. Arabs and Jews and the rest of the world, all under one roof. It gives me hope."

Gabe tussled his son Daniel's hair. His son didn't know anything of the evils of the world. He just wished he could keep it that way.

Gabe and Imbal made their way through the carpets, spices, trinkets, and holiday souvenirs. They didn't buy anything other than some halva for themselves and some chocolate for the kids. Imbal regretted it shortly afterwards as she saw the chocolate covered hands and faces of Daniel and Eliana.

"We need to pop into a Super Pharm and get some baby wipes," Imbal said. The tissues she brought along weren't getting the job done and they were too far from the car.

"There should be one two blocks outside of the old city walls that way," Gabe said, looking at his mobile phone. It had an app for these types of things.

They took the sticky hands in theirs and started walking up the stairs. There were stairs everywhere, with narrow corridors and people on every corner in the old city. They just needed to exit and get into the normal Jerusalem, outside of the city walls.

It took longer than they anticipated. It seemed farther than the app said. They regretted not just washing the kids down with bottled water but it was too late. They opened the doors to Super Pharm and went in.

The air was cold. The lights were bright and everything was pristinely set out. They made their way to the appropriate aisle and picked up the wipes. They didn't linger, but weren't in a rush either.

"Allahu Akbar!"

The voice came from nowhere. Gabe turned his head and the knife went into his neck. Imbal couldn't even scream. She raised her hands and turned to fight, putting herself between her children and the man with a knife.

"Die!" The man was moving in fast motion. He pulled the knife from Gabe's neck and stabbed him again twice in the chest just as Imbal's foot connected with his face. He fell back and got onto his feet immediately.

"Help!" another voice screamed into the street. People turned to look, doe-eyed. A passing police officer saw the panic in the woman's eyes and didn't hesitate. He pushed a button in his car, pulled over, and hit the ground running.

Inside, the terrorist was slashing at Imbal. She crouched low and screamed, "Get back Daniel, get back!" She was distracted as the children rushed towards their dying father. Blood was everywhere. It was all happening so fast. So slow. "Where is everyone?" thought Imbal. "Why aren't they helping us?"

The terrorist lunged at her again, catching her hand. She punched him. As she punched, she got too close and the knife went into her stomach and up her rib cage. Her legs kicked and her fingers scraped at his eyes. He pulled out the knife and then stabbed her three more times, once in the neck, in the eye, and chest.

Blood was everywhere. Daniel and Eliana weren't running.

The terrorist, covered in blood, slipped and reached towards Daniel. He screamed and ran, but the hand held. He was thrown like a rag doll across the room. Eliana just stood and screamed. He picked her up and held the knife to her throat.

By then the policeman was at the door, gun drawn. "Put down the girl!"

"Allahu Akbar!" The knife sliced deep into the baby's flesh just as shots rang out. The policeman shot the terrorist in the head a moment too late. The knife fell to the ground as more soldiers rushed the scene. The pharmacist barely had time to react when it all started and was now next to the fallen girl.

"Bandages! Get me the kit! Call the hospital!" He put pressure on the wound and did his best. The girl was limp in his arms. "Come on!"

Sirens filled the air and the crackle of radios and shouting filled the rest.

"Get the boy! Careful. Is he alive? Just make sure he's breathing. Don't move him!" Shouts were everywhere. Customers had been moved outside and were being interviewed—both for information and to see if they were part of the perpetrators.

"The parents? Someone work on the parents!" The pharmacist was a trained medic and had served in the army. He just wished he had the materials for this. "I don't want to lose anyone!" He shouted at himself as much as anyone else. He didn't let go of the girl. He was her only chance to live.

Just then, the Muezzin was heard over the loud-speakers, calling in the familiar way the faithful Muslims to prayer. It was barely heard inside over the sirens and screams coming from the frantic people trying to keep the four bodies alive.

Chapter Fifteen

SIR JUDD

Sir Barry Judd. Judd liked the sound of that. He would never admit it to anyone and if anyone asked, he would simply scowl and say he was doing his job. *But it does have a nice ring to it,* he thought.

He was given some time off as a reward for Spain. Everyone wanted to have a word with him. He was even approached by sponsors who wanted to use his image to sell their sporting goods. He felt like a superstar.

"Where to, sir?" His driver was instructed by the office to take Judd to the New Forest in the south of England near Southampton to a spa retreat. But he didn't want to presume anything.

"I've never been to one of those spa places. No sense looking a gift horse in the mouth, what?" Judd wasn't used to pampering, but he knew the strain of the last few months had begun taking its toll on him, ever since the sniper's internet postings.

"I understand there'll be some others there as well, sir?"

"It seems that they want to spoil me. I wonder if there'll be a bird waiting for me in my room." Judd had never gotten married. The life of a soldier wasn't easy, and the life of a soldier's wife was worse. By the time he moved to the Met, he was set in his ways. He had the usual suspects he would call and he tried his luck with some women as the opportunity arose, but he wasn't a relationship type and most women weren't the one-night stand type. It put him in an awkward position.

"One can hope, sir." The driver kept his eyes forward. He was used to the bravado from men. From his experience, the ones who talked were never the ones who acted.

They arrived at the New Forest Spa, a boutique hotel set into the woods. The glass and wood worked well; one reflected nature, the other seemed part of it. There was a greeting party, the manager and some press waiting for Judd. He took it all in for what it was—he had become a celebrity.

∞

Jason couldn't sleep or think straight after his encounter with Judd. Part of him wanted to forget the whole thing. There was no way to call off the search for him in the event that Judd was killed. *It would simply compound their efforts*, he thought. *They'd be hunting for the killer of a national hero.*

When he opened his computer, he noticed the headlines on the BBC home page. "*Hero Judd taking a much deserved break*," said the headline. "*After taking the bold move on an anonymous tip, Judd organised and secured the capture and death of the mastermind behind the recent plane bombings. Sources close to Judd recount his extreme disquiet for not taking Timothy Bull alive. Whatever the facts of the case, Superintendent Judd enjoyed the New Forest Spa of...*"

Noting that Judd would be in the same location for three days, Jason had a decision to make. Was it worth it? Would it help or hinder him? Or should he quit while he was ahead. *Most likely it was a trap*, he thought. *This type of information never just leaked; maybe the police were using Judd as bait.*

∞

When the moment came, Judd's reclining body lay on the wooden deck chair next to the hot tub. The summer air had just enough of a breeze to offset the heat of the hot tubs and the full body massage treatments.

"Could I get a beer?" Judd was in a spa but he wasn't going to punish himself.

"Of course, sir. In a bottle or glass? Lager, bitter, ale? Any preference?"

"Local bitter in a glass would be lovely, thanks."

It was still morning, but there was nothing to stop him having a sneaky drink before the rest of the crew joined him. He felt his pocket and pulled out the cigar he had saved. He wasn't a big smoker, but he enjoyed the Partagas No. 4 Cuban cigars given to him by the boys. *Not too much but still enough to give you the kick*, he thought. It came in its own aluminium tube, which acted as a mini humidor, preventing it from drying out too quickly. He pulled it out and enjoyed the feel of it in his fingers. He smelled the earthy leaf that wrapped it. There was no reason to do any of this other than a ritual he had perfected over the years. On the end was a leaf cap and he didn't have a hole-punch or cutter. He sucked on it until the glue released and he removed the leaf cap. The leaves came together with the natural air-waves of the cigar open. It would be a stronger smoke this way but, as he would tell those who watched him from time to time, why else smoke a cigar if not to enjoy it?

He lit the cigar, rolling it as the flame was inhaled into the dried leaves. When it was done, he inspected the glowing end and congratulated himself on a good light. He puffed away contentedly on his wooden deck chair until the waiter returned with his drink. He picked up the drink and moved himself to the hot tub, not more than five paces from his deck chair.

He took off his robe and slid into the hot water. The bubbles were on but not violently so. He was careful to not get his hands wet. He didn't want to ruin his cigar.

"This is the life, isn't it?" he said to himself as much as to the passing massage therapist. She nodded, eyeing the cancer stick in the mouth of the body she was trying to purify.

"Excuse me, can you get m…" His voice was cut off. The therapist's face dropped and she screamed. The waiter came running and stopped dead in his tracks.

"Someone call emergency services," he said. "Someone's shot Judd!"

His head had been flung backwards but the bulk of his body dragged him into the hot water. He slid down, legs powerless to stop him, mind unaware of anything but black. He was floating on his back, blood filling the hot tub. If he were alive, he would have been upset that his cigar got wet.

∞

Jason heard the news shortly after the event. It made the international news and took up a prominent space on BBC's homepage. Tributes were spoken of him in Parliament by the prime minister and countless others, all trying to associate themselves with his now glorious name. Televised newscasts broadcast scenes from the Spanish siege and interview, his role in the capture and killing of the global bombers, and the tragedy of his life being cut short by an assassin's bullet.

We have just heard that they have captured the perpetrator, said the newscaster. *The police have named*

*him as Arthur Dale of no fixed address. When ap-
proached, police officers were fired upon. They
returned fire and killed the suspect. It is thought that
this is the same assassin who killed the secretary of
state earlier this year, as well as the Conservative
party's chief donor, Lord Staines. We anticipate confirmation by the Met office of this later today. In other
news...*

Jason turned off the radio and sat stunned. A copy-cat?

JACK'S BACK

Fred followed the maelstrom of news coverage on the interview from his hotel room in Copenhagen. If he were even just twenty years younger, he would go and find a girl to bring back to his room. As it was, he was feeling every day of his eighty-four years; old, weak, and useless. Betraying Tim was weighing heavily on him. He would die a free man but one who wouldn't warrant even a footnote in history. For who knew that he even existed or was part of the most audacious plan in the history of the world? A plan to jolt the masses into realising that violence was not the answer.

He turned off the television and put on his blazer. He wanted to look respectable as he sat in the café and watched the youth bustle them from one corner to another. He no longer envied the young. He wouldn't mind being young again, but he would miss his life's experiences. His loves, his heartaches, his adventures with the Special Forces. Being relevant. All of this made him who he was. *I forgot to include international terrorist*, he said to himself. He didn't think he had a conscience. *Why do I need to discover it now? Why can't it leave me alone? Like everyone else does...* He battled with his melancholy when alone.

"Mr. Johansen? Fredrick Johansen?"

Startled, Fred looked up. "Yes?"

"My name is Jack. I'm a friend of an old buddy of yours. I was hoping you had some time to talk."

"Of course. Please, have a seat." Fred wasn't alarmed, just pleasantly surprised to have someone want to talk to him. His actions of the last year were the furthest thing from his mind.

"Thanks. Sorry to bother you, but I was passing through the area and noticed from your Facebook that you were in Copenhagen. I hadn't anticipated meeting you so I came straight here."

"My Facebook page? I never thought much about it. Someone put the app on my phone. It must still be active in the background. Did it point you here? At this precise hotel?"

"Amazing what technology can do," Jack said. *With the help from the right type of friends,* he thought.

"Truly amazing," Fred said. "Tell me, how can I help you?" He looked at the young man and his training tried to fit the profile. He couldn't have been more than 31, 35 at the most. He wore a short beard and hair, dressed conservatively but with fine material. Obviously from money. Good teeth and eyes. Not a drunk or drug addict. Good firm handshake. Speaks well and exudes confidence. American, but likely ex-pat.

Jack sat comfortably and waved to the waiter. "May I please have a double espresso with a glass of tap water on the side? Mr. Johansen, anything for you?"

"I'll have a latte with a pastry, something with chocolate. Thank you."

When the waiter left, Jack continued. "I was aware of your friend's work and I admired him from a distance. I actually invested in the venture as well. I was pleased to see it succeed—really, beyond our wildest ambitions."

"Sorry to be a bore, but who are you talking about?"

"Timothy Bull." Jack said the name and waited for the reaction.

Fred went white. "You knew Tim? What do you know about Tim? And me? And what venture or investment are you talking about?" He was starting to think that anonymity was underrated. Who was this guy?

"Tim helped me when I needed it most," Jack said. "Must be nearly nine years ago when I first bumped into him. I won't bore you with the details. Needless to say, I was there when he needed me."

Fred was listening but barely hearing. This Jack character was talking breezily about knowing and being helped by the most hated man in the world.

"We came up with an idea to stop the violence in the world. To throw a spanner into the gears of international trade and industry. I think you know to what I am referring."

Fred started to shake. His betrayal of himself and Tim… for what, to be haunted by this upstart? To be blackmailed? "I think I know what you're talking about," he said eventually.

"Did Tim talk to you about our wider objectives?"

"No. We only had this one mission. To shake the world awake."

"And did you achieve your objective?"

"Not really. All we did was make everyone mad."

"I know. Because you only managed to get the first phase done. And now, because of someone, we won't be able to finish the job."

"Do you know who betrayed us?" Fed tried to say it casually.

"I have a good idea," Jack said. "But that isn't going to help us now. I need to think about how to go forward from here."

"You have more targets?"

Jack didn't answer him. "Did Tim tell you anything about me?"

"Nothing. I didn't know you existed."

"And that's how secrets are kept."

"What do you want with me?"

"To talk. To explain. To tell you a story."

"Story?"

"To let you know how close we came."

Fred was silent.

"I contacted Tim because he was an old friend of my father. My biological father. The same man who betrayed me. But I was able to look past my hatred and hurt and received what he gave me on his death."

"Tim betrayed you?"

"No, my father."

"How did he know Tim?"

"They were stationed together. Worked for their governments against enemies we will never hear about. In their own way, each were heroes."

"And your parents?"

"Heroes of a different sort. From them, I received papers, data, and contacts that took me years to work through. But knowing and acting are two different things. It takes money and intelligence to find your targets and neutralise them."

"And who are the targets?"

"The real people behind the machinery oppressing us. Those who facilitate and promote the systems that crush the spirit and freedom from their citizens. Not all governments and politicians are bad. They are a necessity. We need good government for the simple reason that we need to delegate actions that are too big for us as individuals. Hospitals, schooling, policing, national defence. All are good uses of our collective efforts."

"But you are talking about a system, not people."

"All systems are made of people. Nazi Germany was made up of decent people wrongly directed. Communist Russia was made up of hard working decent people clinging to a false premise. Any dogma that enslaves its people and forces them to continuously sacrifice without return is wrongly directed. I am an optimist. I believe people are generally good. I believe people want to be good. But there are those amongst us who are also genuinely bad. We need to acknowledge that these types of people exist and that they must be removed from circulation by way of incarceration or execution. When those people threaten our existence, they need to be eliminated. As nations, we can't allow others—whether in small groups or as nations—to threaten the peace and security of the world."

"But how does this relate to killing a quarter of a million people and terrorising the world?" Fred didn't see the logic. Maybe there wasn't any.

"Our objective was to demonstrate that security alone would not end violence. Violence is something that could only be eliminated through de-escalation. By reducing the means by which we can hurt each other. By keeping conflicts within nations, allowing them to mature within their own borders. If they wanted to kill each other within their borders, fine. But when they breach their borders, they can no longer claim immunity from retribution. We have reached a point in global history when we need to say that something is right and something is wrong. We can't just muddle along because it may impact trade."

"This is nothing new," Fred said.

"But the message has not been embraced or understood by the population. We need to get the conversation going. Our only hope is for free people to make decisions in the best interest of remaining free. At present, we find ourselves with ever increasing ties to systems—Lilliimption-like—where we are unable to move freely. Shortly after that, our thinking becomes self-censored and we start believing the system. Eventually, we become mere biological extensions of it. We forget that we are our own individuals. We become the system first, and us second."

"And you think blowing up planes achieves this?"

"Not in and of itself. It's part of starting the conversation. When bombs explode, people typically seek shelter. But the first thing they do after that is find and make sure their loved ones are safe. Only then will they go together to find real safety. In our case, the security systems in place short circuit the solution. Instead of finding real safety, they put in place more security systems to supposedly prevent what happened instead of dealing with the underlying causes of the violence or explosions. I want people to start looking at the underlying causes."

"Which are?"

"The suppression of good, hard-working, and honest people. If the salt of the Earth resort to this type of violence, then it's time to rethink the systems that protect us. Naturally, they will point to Tim and myself and you as people who are not salt of the Earth. Just common terrorists. But that would be missing the point. People are angry. Every politician knows this. If we don't resolve the problem, the next step has historically been the guillotine. Since we aren't ruled by monarchs, the politicians' heads will roll."

"A bit of a leap of logic, don't you think?" Fred recalled how he liked the idea when Tim first presented it to him. But thinking and doing were different. Things changed for him after the bombings.

"Let me tell you a story about a group of people who have enormous influence. They aren't elected, yet they control every politician and financial policy maker in the world. They direct the IMF, World Bank, and every central bank, all through impeccable logic. In so doing, have implemented a new global currency for their much sought after new world order. Our second phase of bombings were to target these institutions and the main decision makers behind them. There would be some token politicians, the ones who have set themselves up as defacto dictators under the thinly veiled premise of democracy. But the main actors globally operate in the shadows of secrecy. They are too intelligent to put their head above the parapet to get shot."

Fred listened silently. "Who the hell are you? You seem far too young to be so cynical or to have this type of information at your fingertips."

"I was given three lifetimes of top secret intelligence. I'm as confident as one can be. I was gifted a fortune and given access to illegal slush funds set up during the swashbuckling days of the Cold War. Forgotten monies now utilised to achieve what they were meant to when first put aside. So confidential it was lost in the annals of time."

"I see," Fred said. His body language betrayed his feelings. He felt the impact of his actions. Actions he didn't want to do except for his own cowardice. Looking at this young man across from him, he saw the burning passion of the true believer. *I'm not sure if he's another Bin Laden or just a violent version of Ghandi,* he thought.

Jack noticed Fred's behaviour and stopped lecturing. He pulled out two cigars and flagged the waiter.

"Could we have a bottle of your best Hine Antique brandy, vintage if you have it." Jack looked at Fred. "I assume that's okay with you?"

Fred nodded slowly.

The cigars were good. They moved onto the pavement, away from any potential complainers of their smoke. The chairs were comfortable and overlooked the energetic movement of youth on bicycles and foot.

The city was dynamic, a model example of how government should operate for the people. It had its problems, but it also had many things to its credit.

They smoked in silence, sipping the fine brandy. The cigars lasted almost an hour and their bodies trembled with the hit of nicotine, dulled by the fine alcohol.

As his own cigar finished, Jack got up.

"I think you know what you need to do," Jack said.

Fred nodded.

Jack extended his hand and shook Fred's. "It was good to finally meet you."

Jack turned and walked away. Fred watched him disappear around the corner.

Fred finished his cigar and had as much brandy as he dared. He didn't want to stumble but he knew what he needed to do. He called for the bill but found that Jack had already paid it. He shook his head with a faint smile. He got up and returned to his room.

When the cleaners entered his room the next day, they found him in the bath, dead. The water was a deep red and his skin was white. His head lay back on the tiles. On the desk was a note with one word. *Sorry.*

THE PARK

The air was crisp, the sun shone bright, and all the world was right. Leanne's arm rested gently on Mark's and Sable tried to walk next to them. She pulled on the leash and Mark gave a quick jerk to bring her to heal. Sable tolerated him during times like this. She could barely remember that other place. They didn't treat her badly but her entire life was in a cage. Now she was able to sleep on the sofa, had her own little bed, and unlimited access to food. Mark was always around and this other person was pretty cool. She smelled nice and always had time for her. Sable approved.

The bombings were becoming a memory, however bad. That cold metallic taste of fear was gone. Shops were just beginning to advertise for Christmas. Loud bangs of bin covers no longer caused people to jump. Nerves were less frayed. Just the normal stresses of staying alive, paying the bills, and living life.

"I got a job," Mark said.

"Congratulations! I told you something would come up." Leanne leaned in. She had tried to get him to join her firm but he wanted to keep their personal and business lives separate. She respected the decision but thought it was foolish. They would see much more of each other if they worked together.

"It's not much, but I've been approached by a firm to write my story. They want to do a documentary on me while I write it. I don't know what gets into people's heads but they think it has some human interest element. Rip Van Winkle and all that."

"I'd watch it. Right after the discovery channel, teleshopping, and that show that sets out the best videos on the net."

"Hey!" Mark gave her a friendly push.

"I can't believe how big Sable has grown. She's rippling with muscle. Kinda scary if she wasn't our dog."

"Our dog?"

"Who's dog would she be? She has known me only a day longer than you."

"But she's your dog. No question of that. I'm the go-to in the event that you say no. I'm the pushover."

"Anyway, she loves you. I love you." He kissed her awkwardly. *Why is it so hard to kiss while walking?* he thought.

"I love you too," she said. It was said automatically but she meant it. Mark was the real deal.

He was silent. Sable was behaving herself next to him. Leanne was holding his hand; his arm had grown heavy crooked out to the side, however gallant it looked.

"Do you mind if we let her off the leash? We can sit by the pond and watch the geese." As he asked, he leaned down and clicked the leash. Sable hesitated and then took a couple of steps forward. Convinced of her freedom, she bounded towards the other dogs. She looked large and scary but was really just a muscular marshmallow.

Leanne sat, opening her jacket and settling herself onto the edge of the bench, closest to the arm. Mark remained standing for a bit. He became awkward. When he kneeled instead of sitting next to her, she felt a rush of adrenaline. Her blood shot to her extremities, making her ears hot and fingers tingle. She sat up straighter, looking straight at him. Her eyes involuntarily started to well up. She stayed silent.

"Leanne," Mark said. "My life was given meaning when you entered it. You are my everything. I hope you feel the same because I have an important question to ask you."

Leanne was silent. She felt her head move forward, willing him to ask.

∞

Jeb had been following Leanne for just over a month, establishing patterns of movement and determining the best place to take his shot. He knew that when they went for their walk with that mutt of theirs, they inevitably sat on the same bench. They chatted and fed the ducks and then collected the dog and returned home. It made him sick that she could have such a perfect life when so many of his friends died because of weapons sold to the enemy by her. Today he'd right that wrong.

He also decided that he wasn't going to hide. He'd kill her and walk away. Close up. No chance of missing. He had a silencer but that still made plenty of noise. It wouldn't be pretty. He might get arrested. *Who cares*, he thought. *At least it will be for a cause bigger than me. The park isn't crowded. No reason to get caught.*

He saw the bitch sit down and the loser boyfriend of hers get on his knee. *He's proposing! Poor bastard.* He started walking towards her, hand in his pocket. He pulled out the handgun, a semi-automatic Heckler & Koch Mark 23. It was a bit long and foolish looking with the silencer but it would do the trick.

As he approached, his mind drifted back to his training, his tours, and the mass of killing over there. His stomach muscles clenched but he was otherwise calm. He was ten paces away.

He raised his arm as the gun became an extension of his eyes, and his eyes were on the back of the bitch's head. His finger rested on the trigger.

At that moment, the bitch turned her head and he was looking directly at her. She had beautiful blue eyes and hair that flowed like an angel. Her eyes were full of happy tears and he saw her face go from bliss to terror. His mind instructed his finger to pull the trigger.

∞

"I know we haven't known each other long," Mark said. "But I feel I have known you my entire life. And I can't imagine my life without you."

Mark opened a little box and pulled out a ring. It was a solitaire diamond on a rose gold band. "Leanne, will you marry me?"

Just as she was about to say yes, she noticed Mark's eyes looking over her shoulder. She turned her head and found herself looking down the barrel of some gun. She couldn't move. Time slowed. She wondered if Sable was around and whether she saw this attacker. She wondered whether the ring fit her finger. She remembered where she put her favourite underwear. In the glove compartment. She almost smiled with the memory. She saw the determination on the man's face and looked at him directly in the eyes. She could only see fury. Violence.

∞

Jeb pulled the trigger.

Or he thought he did. Instead, he saw his hand putting the gun back into his pocket. He saw the tears flowing down the bitch's face. He saw the bastard trying to get up. *Probably shit his pants*, he thought to himself.

"I'm a soldier, not a murderer like you," Jeb said. "You'll die, but not by my hand. Not today."

With that, he turned and walked away. Life and death. As simple as that. He saw them grab hold of each other and cry uncontrollably in each other's arms. As he drove away, he couldn't quite put his finger on why he let them live. *I've killed children before for the sins of their parents,* he thought. *But only on order.* He was satisfied with his decision.

MAN ON THE RUN

Jack wondered whether blowing up empty planes would have had the same effect globally. *It would need to be a large number. Three thousand or more*, he thought. But the chances of co-ordinating teams globally to breach security and carry out such an act was beyond his ability. That would require a government or highly organised militia. Regardless, it made him think. The loss of life in June was disgusting. And for what? To be short circuited by a simple betrayal? There must be another way.

He looked at the timetables and destinations of the Trans-Siberian Railway. It was a long distance, but he wanted to cross at the Bering Strait into Alaska. It was insanely dangerous. There was one small chartered flight service that took customers across from the Russian side to America. If he had to, he could try that. But the Trans-Siberian Railway didn't take him to the Bering Straits. It curved into China instead.

"Have you decided, sir?"

The girl behind the window was pleasant. She was beautiful once and still thought of herself as pretty. She looked directly at him with just a hint of a smile. *It wouldn't take much to get her talking*, Jack thought.

"Uh, yes. I'll take a ticket to Skovorodino."

"Wow. That's a long journey. What's there?" she really wanted to have some conversation. Jack used this to his advantage.

"Nothing, but I need to get to Uelen and that's the closest station on this line. I'll need to figure out another way when I get there."

She looked at him carefully. "It's not easy to get where you want to go. You'd be better off to fly." She smiled.

"I'm not too keen on flying lately," Jack said.

"I know. You're not the only one. We've never been so busy." She looked behind her. There was no one next to her either. "Listen, I'm not supposed to tell people this, but there is a way to Uelen. I assume you are talking about Uelen on the Bering Strait?"

Jack nodded.

"My break is in just over half an hour. Can you meet me for a coffee?"

"It would be my pleasure. My treat. Here?"

"No." She said it a bit too quickly. "In the waiting hall just over there." She pointed. Jack looked and nodded. "By the benches."

"I'll be there. How do you like your coffee?"

∞

"Hi, Jack." He handed her a coffee and a white paper bag with a pastry.

"Hi, Valeria." She took the coffee between her hands. "Thanks for waiting for me."

"You piqued my interest. What couldn't you tell me there?"

"I just wanted to know how you were planning to cross to Alaska." She took a sip of coffee.

"Probably by plane but I would love to cross on foot. It's very dangerous. Not sure what I'd do when I get to the other side."

"Aren't you afraid?" she said.

"There are things more scary than cold and ice," Jack said.

Valeria was silent and took another sip of her coffee. "I wouldn't be scared. I'd like to go to America."

Jack had a feeling he knew what was coming next.

"Would you be interested in taking me with you?"

Jack weighed his options. Having a native speaker would help. But she'd be a lot of extra baggage. In the end he decided that life is lived in a constant state of flux. Chaos. That which can't be ordered or made logical. And Valeria was not a logical choice.

"Sure," Jack said. "Why not."

ABOUT THE AUTHOR

Baron was born in Canada.
He currently lives in South East England,
somewhere near the Surry/Sussex borders.
Sightings vary.

If you'd like to follow Baron and receive free samples
of his future writing before it is published, please visit
www.baronalexanderbooks.com